BLOOD BEAST

BY DARREN SHAN

LITTLE, BROWN AND COMPANY

New York   Boston

Little, Brown and Company

Hachette Book Group USA
237 Park Avenue, New York, NY 10017
Visit our Web site at www.lb-teens.com

First U.S. Edition: November 2007

First published in Great Britain by Collins in 2006

Shan, Darren.
    Blood beast / by Darren Shan. — 1st U.S. ed.
        p. cm. — (Demonata ; bk. 5)
    First published: Great Britain : Collins, 2006.
    Summary: When he begins experiencing alarming symptoms at the onset of
the full moon, Grubbs Grady, who has so far escaped his family curse,
fears that he is turning into a werewolf.
    ISBN-13: 978-0-316-00378-0   ISBN-10: 0-316-00378-6
    [1. Demonology—Fiction. 2. Werewolves—Fiction. 3. Horror stories.]
I. Title.
    PZ7.S52823Bl 2007
    [Fic]— dc22

                                        2007028108

                        10 9 8 7 6 5 4 3 2 1

                                RRD-C

                Printed in the United States of America

✠ ✠ ✠

For:
Mary Barry (my gruesome Granny),
who overcame a much fiercer beast than any Grubbs Grady
ever faced! Glad to still have you with us, old 'un!!!

OBEs (Order of the Bloody Entrails) to:
Catherine "the cutthroat" Holmes
Katie McGowan — there's a new killer kid on the block!

Mage superior:
Stella "the gouger" Paskins

Magical support:
Christopher Little's circular crew

PART ONE

✠ ✠ ✠

ŁOCH

DAMN THE SANDMAN

✚ ✚ ✚

MY hands are red with blood. I'm running through a forest. Naked, but I don't care. I'm an animal, not a human. Animals don't need clothes.

Blood on my tongue too. Must have fed recently. Can't remember if it was a wild creature or a person. Not bothered much either way. Still hungry — that's all that matters. Need to find something new to chew. And soon.

I leap over a fallen log. As I land, my bare feet hit twigs. They snap and I sink into a pool of mud. I collapse, howling. The twigs bite into me. I catch a glimpse of fiery red eyes, peering up out of the mud. They aren't twigs — they're teeth! I lash out with my feet, screaming wordlessly . . .

. . . and mud and pieces of bark fly everywhere. I stare at the mess suspiciously, my heart rate returning to normal. I was wrong. I haven't fallen victim to a monstrous baby with mouths in the palms of its hands and balls of fire where its eyes should be. It's just a muddy hole, covered with the remains of branches and leaves.

Scowling, I rise and wipe my feet clean on clumps of nearby grass. As I'm using my nails to pick off some splinters, a voice calls, *"Grubbs . . ."*

The name doesn't register immediately. Then I remember — that's *my* name. Or it used to be, once upon a time. I glance up warily, sniffing the air, but all I can smell is blood.

"Grubitsch . . ." the voice murmurs, and I growl angrily. I hate my real name. Grubbs isn't great, but it's better than Grubitsch. Nobody ever called me that except Mom and my sister, Gret.

"You can't find me," the voice teases.

I roar into the darkness of the forest, then lurch at the bushes where I think the voice is coming from. I tear through them, but there's nothing on the other side.

"Wrong," the voice laughs, coming from somewhere behind me.

I whirl and squint, but I can't see anyone.

"Over here," the voice whispers. This time it's coming from my right.

Still squinting, I edge closer towards the source of the voice. This feels wrong, like it's a trap. But I can't back away from it. I'm drawn on by curiosity, but also something else. It's a girl's voice, and I think I know whose it is.

Movement to my left, just as I'm about to round a tree. Eight long, pale arms wave in the light of the moon. Dozens of tiny snakes hiss and slither. I cry out with fear and slam into the tree, shielding my eyes from the horror. Seconds pass but nothing attacks. Lowering my arms, I realize the arms were just branches of a couple of neighboring trees. The snakes were vines, blowing in the wind.

I feel sick but I force a weak chuckle, then slide around the tree, in search of the person who called to me.

I'm at the edge of a pond. I frown at it. I know this forest, and there should be no pond here. But there it lies regardless, the full moon reflected in its still surface. I'm thirsty. The blood has dried on my tongue, leaving a nasty copper-like taste. I crouch to drink from the pond, going down on all fours and lowering my head to the water like a wolf.

I see my face in the mirrorlike water before I drink. Blood everywhere, caked into my flesh and hair. My eyes widen and fill with fear. Not because of the blood, but because I can see the shadow of somebody behind me.

I start to turn but it's too late. The girl pushes my head down hard and I go under. Water fills my mouth and I gag. I try to fight but the girl is strong. She holds me down and my lungs fill. The coppery taste is still there and I realize, as I blink with horrified fascination, that the pond is actually a pool of blood.

As my body goes limp, the girl pulls me up by my hair and laughs shrilly as I draw a hasty, terrified breath. *"You always were a useless coward, Grubitsch,"* she sneers.

"Gret?" I moan, staring up at the mocking smile of my sister. "I thought you were dead."

"No," she croaks, eyes narrowing and snout lengthening. *"You are."*

I weep as her face transforms into that of a mutant wolf. I want to run or hit her but I can only sit and stare. Then, as the transformation ends, she opens her mouth wide and howls. Her head shoots forward. Her fangs fasten around my throat. She bites.

✠ ✠ ✠

✠ I wake choking. I want to scream, but in my imagination Gret's teeth are locked around my throat. I lash out at my dead sister, still half in the dreamworld. When my arm fails to connect, I rub at my eyes, and my bedroom swims back into sight around me.

Groaning softly, I sit up and dangle my legs over the edge of the bed. Covering my face with my hands, I recall the worst parts of the dream, then shiver and get up to go to the bathroom. No point trying to sleep again tonight. I know from past experience that the nightmares will be even worse if I do.

I pause in the doorway of the bathroom, suddenly certain that demons are lurking in the shadows. If I turn on the light, they'll attack. I know it's ridiculous, a ripple from the nightmare, but despite that, my finger trembles in the air by the switch, refusing to press.

"The hell with it," I finally sigh, stepping forward. Letting my fear have its way, on this night, as on so many others, I go about my business in the dark.

MISERY

✠   ✠   ✠

Of course I have nightmares — who doesn't?"

"Every night?"

"No."

"Most nights?"

A pause. "No."

"But a lot?"

I shrug and look away. I'm in Mr. Mauch's office. Misery Mauch, the school guidance counselor. He holds court a few times a week. Chats with students who are struggling with homework, peer pressure, pushy parents. Normal kids with normal problems.

And then there's me.

Misery *loves* sitting down for a warts 'n' all session with *me*.

Why wouldn't he? Everyone here knows the Grubbs Grady story — parents and sister slaughtered in front of him . . . long months locked up in a nuthouse ("incarcerated in a facility for the temporarily disturbed," Misery puts it) . . . came to Carcery Vale to live in a spooky old house with his uncle Dervish . . . that uncle lost his marbles soon after . . . Grubbs played nurse for a year until he recovered . . . went to a movie set with Dervish and his friend Bill-E Spleen months later . . . witnessed the tragic deaths of hundreds of people when a disastrous fire burned the set to the ground.

With a history like that, I'm a dinosaur-sized bone for every psychiatric dog within a hundred-mile radius!

"Would you like to tell me about your dreams, Grubitsch?" Misery asks.

"No."

"Are you sure?"

I feel like laughing but don't. Misery's harmless. It can't be much fun, trekking around his small collection of schools, dealing with the same boring teenage problems day after day, year after year. If I were in his shoes, I'd be itching to get my hands on a juicily messed-up student like me too.

"Grubitsch?" Misery prods after a few seconds of silence.

"Hmm?"

"Telling me about your dreams might help. A problem shared is a problem halved."

I almost respond with, "What's a cliché shared?" but again I hold my tongue. I'd ruin Misery's day if I cut him down like that. Might reduce him to tears.

"They're not much of a problem, sir," I say instead, trying to wind the session down. I'm missing physics and I actually like that class.

"Please, Grubitsch, call me William."

"Sorry, sir — I mean, William."

Misery smiles big, as if he's made a breakthrough. "The

nightmares must be a problem if they're not going away," he presses gently. "If you told me, perhaps we could find a way to stop them."

"I don't think so," I respond, a bit sharper than I meant. He's talking about stuff that is way over his head. I don't mind a school counselor showing interest in me, but I dislike the way he's acting like a second-rate mind-sleuth, clumsily trying to draw out my secrets.

"I didn't mean to offend you, Grubitsch," Misery says quickly, realizing he's stepped over the line.

"To be honest, *sir*," I say stiffly, "I don't think you're qualified to discuss matters like this."

"No, no, of course not," Misery agrees, his features sorrowing up. "I don't want to pretend to be something I'm not. I apologize if I gave that impression. I only thought, if you were in the mood to talk, it might help. It might be a beginning. Of course it's not my . . . I'm under no illusion . . . like you said, I'm not qualified to . . ." He mutters to a halt.

"Don't have a breakdown," I laugh, feeling guilty. "It's no biggie. I just don't want to talk about my dreams to anyone. Not right now."

Misery gulps, nods sharply, then says I can go. Tells me he'll be back next week but won't ask to see me. He'll give me some space. Maybe, in a month or two, he'll call me in again, to "shoot the breeze."

I hesitate at the door, not wanting to leave him on such a down note — his head's bowed over his notes and he looks like he's fighting back tears.

"Mr. Mau — William." He looks up curiously. "Next time, if you want, you can call me Grubbs."

"*Grubbs?*" he repeats uncertainly.

"It's what my friends call me."

"Oh," he says, and his face lights up like he's won the lottery.

I slip out, masking a smile. Guidance counselors — child's play!

✠ Lunch. Loch wants to know what I was talking with Misery about.

"The size of your brain," I tell him. "We wondered how small it was."

"Don't worry about the size of *my* brain," Loch snorts. "My brain's fine. A lot healthier than your pea of a think tank."

"How big *is* a brain?" Charlie asks. Everyone stares at him. "I mean, does it fill up the whole head?" He starts poking his skull, searching for soft spots.

"In your case, I doubt it," Loch says. "You've probably got enough empty space in there to hold a soccer ball."

Laughter all around. Even Charlie laughs. He's used to being the butt of our jokes. He doesn't mind. They're always lighthearted. Everyone likes Charlie Rall. He's too nice to be mean to.

Six of us, finding cover from the rain in a doorway overlooking the soccer field. The usual pack of barbarians are kicking the life out of a tired old ball — and each other — on the field, oblivious to the rain.

My group — me, Loch, Charlie, Frank, Leon, and Mary. Loch and I stand a head or more above any of the others. We're the biggest pair of hulks in our school, which is what drew us to each other in the first place. Loch's a wrestler.

He wanted me to be his partner, so he became my friend. I held out for a long time — real wrestling's nothing like the stuff on TV, very calculated and unspectacular — but he eventually persuaded me to try it. I'm not very good and don't get a real kick out of it, but to keep Loch happy I travel to a few meets every month and get down 'n' sweaty on the mats.

"I think Misery's sexy in an older man kind of way," Mary says to a chorus of astonished jeers and catcalls.

"You've got the hots for *Mauch*?" Leon gasps, faking a heart attack.

"No," Mary says coolly. "I just think he's sexy. I bet women are all over him outside school hours."

The laughter dies away and the five testosteronetastic guys in the group look at one another uncertainly. It's not something we'd admit to, but girls our age know a hell of a lot more about the adult world than we do. Adults operate differently. It's easy to tell the winners and losers in school, the cools and geeks. But the world beyond is puzzling. Professional athletes are obviously cool, and so are actors, rock stars, and so on. But what about normal guys? What makes an ordinary man attractive to a woman? I don't know. But if Misery Mauch has *it*, we could all be in trouble later on. By their frowns, I know the others are thinking exactly the same thing.

While we're trying to come to terms with a world where Misery Mauch is a sex god, Reni and Shannon saunter up, arm in arm, laughing at some private joke.

"I was just telling the boys," Mary says, "how sexy Mr. Mauch is."

"William?" Reni says, nodding thoughtfully. "He's a hottie."

"*William?*" Loch barks at his sister.

"That's what he told me to call him."

"I didn't know you'd been seeing the counselor," Loch growls.

"There's a lot you don't know about me," Reni says mysteriously, then raises an eyebrow at Shannon. "William Mauch — dull or dreamy?"

"Deliciously dreamy," Shannon says seriously — then laughs. "I'm sorry! Your faces!"

"Cows," Leon snaps as the other girls squeal along with Shannon. "That wasn't funny."

"It was hilarious," Reni counters, crying with laughter. "You guys are so easy to wind up. Imagine Misery Mauch as eye candy!" She laughs even harder.

"Here," I say, pulling out a handkerchief and handing it to Reni.

Reni smiles sweetly and dabs at her cheeks with the hankie. Four sets of lips immediately purse — wolf whistles galore.

"Grubbs and Reni sitting in a tree . . ." sings Frank.

"Screw you," I grunt, and coolly retrieve my handkerchief from Reni — cue more whistles.

✠ Lunch flies by as it usually does. So much to talk about — friends, teachers, homework, TV, movies, computer games, music, wrestling, the size of brains. Robbie McCarthy joins us halfway through. He's not a regular member of the gang, but he's been cuddling up to Mary recently, so he's had to spend time with the rest of us.

I joke around with Reni a lot. The handkerchief was especially for her. One of Dervish's. I use tissues, like everybody else who isn't living in the Middle Ages. I've been carrying it around for a week, waiting for a chance to present it to her. Corny, and done as a joke — but half serious too. A chance to share a smile and a sweet look.

Reni knows I like her. And I think she's hot for the Grubbster. But I haven't had much experience in things like this. There's every chance I've read the signals wrong. I won't know for sure until I find the guts to put an arm around her and try for a kiss, but I think the odds are in my favor.

Loch's cool with it. I've seen how he is with other guys who put the moves on Reni — he puffs himself out to look even bigger than he already is and growls like a bear, scaring them away. If Reni was keen on any of them, she'd tell him to back off. But most of the time she lets him play the protective big brother and even encourages it.

It's important to have Loch's approval. He's my best friend. You don't try to date your best friend's sister without his permission. It just isn't done.

✠ Towards the end of lunch, a small, chubby boy with a lazy left eye shuffles over and I feel a stab of guilt, much stronger than the pang I felt in Misery Mauch's office.

"Hi, Grubbs," Bill-E says, smiling hopefully.

"Hi," I grunt.

"Hey, Bill-E! How's my man?" Loch exclaims, and sticks his hand out. Bill-E extends his own hand automatically, but Loch whips his away, puts his thumb on his nose, sticks his tongue out, and wiggles his fingers. "Sucker!"

Bill-E flushes but manages a sick grin and lowers his hand sheepishly.

"Very mature," Reni says drily, rolling her eyes at her brother.

"The shrimp doesn't mind, do you, Spleen?" Loch chortles, grabbing Bill-E's head in a wrestling lock.

"No," Bill-E says, voice muffled. Loch releases Bill-E and ruffles his hair. Bill-E's still smiling but the smile's *very* strained and his face is fire engine red. "How you doing, Grubbs?"

"Not bad. You?"

"OK."

We smile awkwardly at each other. The rest of the group stare at us for a second. Then normal conversation resumes, only we're cut out of it.

"Doing anything this weekend?" Bill-E asks.

"Not a lot. Maybe practicing some wrestling moves with Loch."

"Oh. I was thinking of coming over to watch some movies . . . if that's OK. . . ."

"Hell, you don't have to ask." I laugh uneasily. "You can drop in any time you want. It's your house as much as mine."

"Coolio!" Bill-E's smile resumes its normal shape. "You want to watch a movie with me?"

"Maybe. But I might have to go over to Loch's and practice. You know."

"Yeah," Bill-E says quietly. "I know."

The bell rings and everyone files back to class. Hundreds of kids groaning, shouting, laughing. Bill-E heads off in his own direction. He doesn't say goodbye. I watch him walk alone and lonely in the crowd and I feel twisted and vile, like something a maggot would crawl out of its way to avoid.

Bill-E Spleen was my best friend before Loch Gossel hit the scene. When I moved here after my parents' death and my trip to the nuthouse, he made me feel like I wasn't all by myself in the world. He helped me establish a life again. Settled me in at school, kept me company during lunch when everybody else was wary of me. Fought by my side on the *Slawter* film set — and it wasn't fire we had to contend with. Tried to help when my nightmares kicked back in hard not long afterwards, even though his own mind was in turmoil.

How do I repay him? By abandoning him for the friendship of Loch, Reni, and our little group. Cutting him loose. Being a Judas.

It's wrong, but it's the way things go. When an old friend doesn't fit in with your new pals, you cut him loose. It's the law of school. I've dumped other friends in the past, and several have done it to me. The difference here is that Bill-E's my half brother. Even though he doesn't know it.

✠ Chemistry. I usually find it interesting, but this afternoon I can't concentrate. I keep thinking about Bill-E. I didn't mean to give him the big brush-off. When I first met Loch, I had time for Bill-E. I'd only see Loch occasionally after school. I still hung out with Bill-E a lot.

That gradually changed. Loch began inviting me around to his house and coming over to mine. Through Loch I became friends with Frank Martin, Charlie Rall, and Leon Penn. And through them I got to know Shannon Campbell and Mary Hayes — and, of course, Reni.

Reni makes me forget about Bill-E for a few minutes. Daydreaming about her shoulder-length auburn hair, long eyelashes, light brown eyes, her curves . . . She's not perfect by any means — big and sturdy like her brother, with a ski-slope of a nose — but everybody thinks she's one of the hottest girls in our school.

I shake my head to stop thinking about Reni and my thoughts drift back to Bill-E. All those new friends made demands. It was exciting to be accepted by them, included in their conversation, treated as an equal. It had been a long time since I was part of a crowd. I hadn't realized how much that mattered to me, or how much I'd missed it.

I wanted Bill-E to hang out with us but he just didn't fit in. I'm not sure why. He's younger than most of us — he started school a year early — but Leon isn't a lot older than him. He's small, but Frank's no giant either. He uses corny words like "Coolio!" but Robbie's favorite exclamation is the seriously uncool "Radical!" He has a lazy eye, but Charlie has buckteeth, Shannon has an ugly facial mole, I'm built like the Hulk. . . . We're all a bit weird, one way or another.

Bill-E is smart, funny, a much better talker than me. But he never found a niche at school. I didn't realize it when I first started. Bill-E seemed like the most normal kid around. I knew he didn't have a lot of friends, but I was sure he fit in better than I did.

After a while I began to notice things. Like how Bill-E never went to anybody's house after school. How people made jokes about him and aped him when he said things like "Coolio!" How he was bullied by boys like Loch Gossel.

I'm not blind to how Loch treats Bill-E. He teases him all

the time, like with the fake handshake and headlock today. It's different from the way he treats Charlie. Nastier. He embarrasses Bill-E in front of others, makes him feel small and unwanted.

I often thought of challenging Loch and the others who pick on Bill-E. If any of them hurt him, I'd have definitely taken them on. But teasing is harder to deal with. You can't punch a guy for being sarcastic to somebody . . . can you?

I'd have worsened the situation if I'd interfered, made Bill-E look like a weakling who couldn't stand up for himself. Besides, it wasn't so bad. His life wasn't a walking misery. And he always had *me* to cheer him up.

Class ends. English next. I walk to it by myself, quiet, thoughtful.

I feel ashamed. I should go up to Bill-E this afternoon. Invite him back to my place. Free the weekend up to hang out with him. Watch movies, eat popcorn, go searching for Lord Sheftree's buried treasure. Like we used to.

But I won't. Instead I'll just put up with the guilt, wait for it to pass, then let things go on as they have been. Lousy, yeah, but that's the way it is. Misery Mauch wouldn't understand if I tried to explain, but I'm sure anyone else in the school — or any school in the world — would.

NIGHTMARES

✠ ✠ ✠

OF course I have nightmares — who doesn't?"

I brushed Misery off with that line, but it followed me home from school like a stray dog. I live a couple of miles outside Carcery Vale, in a massive old house, three floors high, filled with antiques and mystical knickknacks. It was once the property of a tyrant named Lord Sheftree, a charming guy who enjoyed chopping up babies into little pieces and feeding them to his pet piranha. But these days it belongs to my uncle, Dervish Grady — as rich as Lord Sheftree, and much more powerful, but without any of the nasty habits.

Dervish is munching on a sandwich in the kitchen when I get home. "Good day at school?" he asks, handing me half of the sandwich.

"So-so," I reply, taking a bite. Chicken and bacon. Yum!

Dervish looks much the same as when I first met him. Thin, tall, bald on top, grey around the sides. A tight grey beard that he shaved off a year or so ago but has grown back.

Piercing blue eyes. Dressed all in denim. The only real difference is his expression. His face is more lined than it used to be, and he has the look of a man still recovering from a haunting. Which he is.

"Bill-E said he might come over this weekend," I tell him.

Dervish nods and goes on chewing. He knows things aren't the same between Bill-E and me but he's never said anything. I guess he doesn't think there's any point — nothing he says could fix the situation. It's best for adults to keep out of things like this. It's widely accepted that we can't solve their problems, so I'll never understand why so many of them think they can solve ours.

I tell Dervish about my session with Misery. He's only mildly interested. "Mauch is a nice guy," he says, "but not too bright. If he gets too inquisitive, let me know and I'll speak to him."

"It'll be a cold day in hell when I can't handle the likes of Misery Mauch myself," I snort.

"Oh, Grubbs, you're so manly!" Dervish gushes, fluttering his eyelids.

"Get stuffed!" I grunt.

We laugh and finish the sandwich.

✠ "Of course I have nightmares — who doesn't?"

I can't get the damn line out of my head! All the way through doing my homework, while watching TV, then listening to CDs and flicking through a wrestling magazine of Loch's.

Everyone has nightmares, sure, but I doubt if many people have nightmares like *mine*. Delirious dreams of demons, wholesale slaughter, a universe of webs and comet-sized monsters. All based on firsthand experience.

I go to bed about 11:30, fairly normal for me, but sleep doesn't come easily. And when it does . . .

I'm in my bedroom at home — my first home. Blood seeps from the eyes of the soccer players in the posters on my walls, but that doesn't bother me. Gret walks in. She's been split in two down the back. Guts trail behind her. A demon with a dog's body and a crocodile's head is chewing on her entrails.

"Dad wants you," Gret says.

"Am I in trouble?" I ask.

"Not as much as me." She sighs.

Down the hall to Mom and Dad's room. I've walked this a thousand times in my nightmares, always feeling the heat and fear. A few tears trickle down my cheeks as my hand rests on the doorknob, the way they always do. I know what I'm going to find inside — my parents, dead, and a wickedly smug Lord Loss. I don't want to open the door, but of course I do, and everything happens the way it did that night when my world first fell apart.

The scene shifts and I'm in the insane asylum. Arms bound, howling at the walls, seeing imaginary demons everywhere I look. Then one of the walls fades away. It turns into a barrier of webs. Dervish picks his way through them. "I know demons are real," he says. "I can help you."

"Help me escape?" I sob.

"No." He holds up a mirror, and I see that I've turned into a werewolf. "Help you die," he snarls, and swings at my neck with an axe.

I kick the covers off and roll out of bed. I hit the floor hard and scramble a few yards across it, fleeing my axe-wielding uncle. Then my vision clears and I realize that I'm awake. Groaning, I push myself to my feet and check my clock. Nearly one in the morning. Looks like I won't be getting any decent sleep tonight either.

My T-shirt and boxers are soaked through with sweat. I change, go into the bathroom, splash cold water over my face, then go to walk around the mansion. I often stroll when I can't sleep, exploring the warren of hallways and rooms, safe here, knowing no harm can befall me. This house is protected by powerful spells.

Creeping through the old, restored part of the mansion, feet cold from the stone floors, too lazy to go back and get my slippers. I find myself in the newer section, an eyesore that was tacked on to the original shell when it was uninhabitable. Dervish keeps talking about demolishing the extension, but he hasn't gotten around to it yet.

I return to the ornate, overblown majesty of the older building and wind up in the hall of portraits, as I usually do on sleepless nights like this. Dozens of paintings and photographs, all of dead family members. Many are of young people, cut down long before their natural time — like my sister, Gret.

I study Gret's photo for ages, a lump in my throat, wishing for the millionth time that I could tell her how sorry I am that I wasn't there for her in her hour of need — her hour of lycanthropy.

It's the family curse. Lots of us turn into werewolves. It's been in the bloodline for more generations than anyone can remember. It strikes in adolescence. Loads of us hit twelve, thirteen . . . maybe even seventeen or eighteen . . . and *change*. Our bodies alter. We lose our minds. Become savage beasts who live to kill.

We're not werewolves like in the movies, who change when the moon is round and then resume our normal forms. When the change hits, it's forever. The victim has a few months before the final fall, when he or she goes a bit nutso each full moon. But then the night of total change sweeps in, and there's no way back after that. Except one. The way of Lord Loss and demons.

✠ Dervish's study. Playing chess against myself on the computer. The study's an enormous room, even by the mansion's grand standards. Unlike the other rooms in the old quarters, it's carpeted, the walls covered with leather panels. There are two huge desks, several bookcases, a PC, laptop, typewriter. Swords, axes, and other weapons hang from the walls. Dervish removed them when he was prone to sleepwalking and attacking me in his sleep. He's safe as a baby now, so the weapons are back. But he never replaced the five chess boards he once kept here, which is why I'm playing on the computer.

Gret was infected with the family curse. In an attempt to save her, Mom and Dad locked horns with a demon master named Lord Loss. Yeah, this isn't just a world of werewolves — demons also prowl the shadowy corridors of the night. The Demonata, to give them their full title.

Lord Loss is a horrible creature with lumpy pale red flesh and a snake-filled hole where his heart should be. He's always bleeding from thousands of small cuts and cracks in his skin, and he floats around instead of walking. He thrives on pain. Haunts sad, tortured humans, feeding on their misery. Nothing appeals to him more than a person in severe agony — except maybe a cracking game of chess.

My hand moves slowly on the mouse, directing black and white pieces on the screen. A powerful family magician discovered Lord Loss's passion for chess many decades ago. He established a contest wherein two relatives of an affected child could challenge the demon master to a chess match. If Lord Loss was defeated, he'd restore the child's natural form and lift the curse forever. But if he won . . .

My parents lost. Under Lord Loss's rules, both were killed, along with Gret. I would have died too, but I was able to call upon hidden magical powers and escape.

Months later, under Dervish's care, I learned the truth about what happened, and that Bill-E was my secret half brother. I also found out that Bill-E had fallen prey to the lycanthropic curse.

Dervish and I faced Lord Loss. It was the bravest, most terrifying thing I've ever done or hope to do. I managed to outfox Lord Loss and turn his love of misery against him. He didn't take it lightly. Swore revenge on all three of us.

He almost extracted that revenge months later on the set of a movie called *Slawter.* A horror maestro was making a film about demons. Dervish, Bill-E, and I were lured into a trap. Lord Loss set an army of demons loose on the cast and crew. Hundreds of people died horribly, but we managed to escape.

Bill-E was badly shaken by his encounter with demons. With Dervish's help he recovered and is back to his old self, pretty much. But there's a nervousness in his look these days — he's always watching the shadows for flickers of demons.

And me? Apart from the nightmares and sleepless nights, have I gotten over it? Am I living the good life, getting on with things, making my way in the world? Well, yes, I'm trying. But there are a couple of flies in the ointment of my life, threatening to mess everything up.

First, it'll be a few more years before I know for sure whether or not I carry the lycanthropic gene. There's a strong possibility I could turn into a werewolf.

If I do start to turn, I'm damned. Lord Loss won't intervene. He hates us with an inhuman passion. Nothing in either universe would tempt him to offer me the chance of salvation. Dervish hasn't said as much but we both know the score — if I fall under the spell of the moon and my body changes, an axe to the neck will be the only cure.

As for the second fly . . . well, in a way that's even worse than the first.

Back in my bathroom, I splash more water over my face. Letting myself drip-dry, I study the water flowing down the drain. It spirals out of the sink in a counterclockwise direction, under the control of gravity. I focus and stare hard at the water. An inner force grows at my will. The stream of water sputters, then starts to spiral downwards smoothly again — but in a *clockwise* direction.

I watch for a few seconds, then shake my head and break the spell. The flow of water returns to normal. I head back to bed, dejected and scared, to spend the rest of the night awake and miserable beneath the covers.

Magicians are rare. Only one or two are born every century, humans with the magical potential of demons, who can change the world with the flick of a wrist.

There are others called mages. They can perform magic when there's demonic energy in the air, but under everyday conditions they can only manage minor spells. Most mages are part of a group known as the Disciples — they fight demons and try to stop them from crossing over to our world.

As far as anyone knows, I'm neither a magician nor a mage. I have more magical ability than most people, and tapped into it when I faced Lord Loss and his familiars. But I'm not a true part of the world of magic.

That suits me just fine. I don't want to become a demon-battling Disciple. I want to lead an ordinary life. The thought of brushing shoulders with Lord Loss or his kind again terrifies me. And as somebody who isn't naturally magical, there's no reason why I should get involved in any more demonic battles. I can sit on the sidelines with the rest of humanity, ignorant of the wars being fought between the forces of good and evil, free of the curse of magic and the responsibilities it brings.

At least that's what Dervish believes. That's how I'd *like* it to be.

But something changed in *Slawter*. I discovered a power within myself, and although I hid it from Dervish, it hasn't gone away. These past few months, I've found myself doing things I shouldn't be able to. The magic is working its way out, eager to break free. It allows me to reverse the flow of water, lift great weights, move objects without touching them. I've awoken several times to find myself levitating above my bed.

I've fought the magic with desperate determination. And for the most part I've been successful. I hope that by focusing and fighting it every step of the way, I can work it out of my system and return to normal.

I'd like to talk with Dervish about it and seek his advice. But I'm afraid. Magic is his life. He's a Disciple first and foremost, dedicated to the task of keeping the world safe from demons. Dervish loves me but I have no doubt that, if he knew about my power, he'd press me into learning more spells. He'd say the world needed me. He'd nag, lecture, and plead. I'd resist, but my uncle can be extremely persuasive when he puts his mind to it. I'm certain he'd nudge me back into the world of magic . . . back into the world of demons.

So here I am. I want to be an average teenager whose only worries are puberty, acne, scoring with girls, impressing my friends, and getting through school in one piece. But I'm forced to spend the better part of every day brooding about turning into a werewolf or becoming a whiz kid wizard who has to fight evil, heartless demons.

"Of course I have nightmares. . . ."

PREPARATIONS

✠   ✠   ✠

DERVISH has to go away for a couple of days. "Meera's heading off for distant pastures, might not be back in our neck of the woods for several months, wants to say goodbye in style."

"'In style'?" I smirk. Meera Flame is one of Dervish's closest friends. Definitely his sexiest. She's hotter than a hot dog that's been cooked extra-*hot!* "Are you and Meera finally going to get it on?"

"Don't be ridiculous," Dervish snorts. "We're just friends. You know that."

"That's what you always *tell* me . . ." I tease.

"Well," Dervish huffs, "it's true. I've never made a pass at her and I don't intend to start now."

"Why not?" I ask, genuinely interested.

Dervish pulls a saintly expression. "Grubbs," he says softly. "Remember when I told you that your dad was Bill-E's Dad too?"

"Yes . . ." Warily.

"What I didn't tell you was that your mother . . . well, the woman you thought of as your mom only met your dad after you were born. Meera . . ." He stops.

I gape at him, head pounding, limbs trembling. My world starts to explode.

Then I catch his grin.

"You son of a jackal!" I roar, smacking his balding head. "That wasn't funny."

"Oh, it so was," he laughs, wiping away tears.

Most of the time I get a kick out of Dervish's warped sense of humor. But there are other times when it really gets to me.

"Keep it up," I growl. "Maybe I'll tell Misery Mauch about you. I doubt if he'd see the funny side of a sick joke like that. Wouldn't surprise me if he took me out of your custody and put me someplace where the people are halfway normal."

"If only." Dervish sighs, then squints at me. "I don't want to lay it on heavy, but I've got something to say and I want you to pay attention."

"What now?" I ask with a sulky sneer. "Ma and Pa Spleen are my grandparents? Misery Mauch is your long-lost brother?"

"This house has been wrecked once already," Dervish says. "I don't want it destroyed again. Keep your freakish little friends under as much control as you can. A certain amount of wear and tear is unavoidable, I accept that, but they'll only run wild if you let them. Lay down the law and they won't cause too much damage. And for heaven's sake, don't let any of them into my study. Remember that it's

guarded by spells, so if anyone wanders in there unin-
vited . . ."

"What are you babbling about?" I snap. I hate when he
starts on a spiel without making it clear what the subject is.

Dervish frowns. "A bit slow today, aren't you?"

"*What?*" I roar impatiently.

"I'm going away." He raps my head with his knuckles.
"You'll have the house to yourself." He raps it again. "It's the
weekend."

He goes to rap my head a third time. I catch his hand in
midair, my face lighting up with a smile as I finally get it. At
the exact same moment we exclaim, me excitedly, Dervish
sarcastically —

"*Paaarteeeeeee!*"

"Strip poker," Frank says earnestly. "It's a must."

"Hey!" Loch barks. "My sister will be there."

"So we'll wait till she sneaks off with Grubbs, then . . . *ba-
da-boom!*"

Everybody laughs, even Loch.

"Have you told the girls yet?" Charlie asks.

"No. I wanted to discuss it with you all first, get some
ideas, like how many people to invite, if I should have a
theme, if —"

"*Theme?*" Loch snorts. "This isn't a fancy dress party, fool!"

"I wouldn't invite too many," Leon says, a worried look
on his face. "I made that mistake once. Had just about the
whole school at my place while my parents were away skiing.
I did what I could to clean up the next day, but it was impossible."

"Yeah," Frank nods. "This is your first party. You don't want to blow it by taking on more than you can handle."

"Especially since there's so much opportunity for the future," Loch agrees. "That mansion could be highly valuable over the next few years. Loads of rooms — loads of *bedrooms* — and an uncle who knows the score. . . . It's a gold mine. But we've got to be careful. If we trash the house now, Dervish might never leave you alone again."

The discussion continues. Everyone — Loch, Frank, Charlie, Leon, and Robbie — chips in with their own ideas. Music, food, drink, the guest list . . . each is debated at great length. But the guest list is the one we keep coming back to, the topic that creates the most divisions.

"Two girls to each guy," Frank insists. "If not three."

"Nah," Robbie grunts. "Equal numbers, or else they'll gang up on us."

"What do you care?" Leon challenges him. "You only have eyes for Mary."

Robbie winks. "A lot can happen at a party."

Out of the blue, Charlie shouts, "Jelly beans. You've got to have jelly beans. Plates of them everywhere."

"*You're* a bloody jelly bean!" Loch roars as we fall apart in tears of laughter.

"What are you hyenas splitting your sides about now?" Reni asks, appearing on the scene without warning, Shannon by her side.

"We're —" Charlie starts.

Loch elbows him and nods sharply at me — my party, my news.

"Dervish is away this weekend," I tell Reni, wishing my

heart wouldn't throb so loudly — I'm sure she can hear it. "I'm having a party."

"Great," Reni smiles. "I hope we're invited?"

"Of course," I say miles too quickly. Then, aiming for cool, "But don't tell anyone. I want to keep it exclusive — just a select handful of my more discerning acquaintances."

"Nice," Reni says, and strides away, sharing a giggle with Shannon.

"'More discerning acquaintances,'" Leon mimics as the others poke me in the ribs and make catcalls. "You're full of it sometimes, Grady."

✠ Word spreads quickly about the party. I've never been so popular, surrounded before and after classes, pumped for details, besieged with requests for an invite. I think the location of the party is as much of a draw as anything else. Everyone in the Vale knows about the spooky old mansion where I live, but most people have never been inside.

At lunch I'm faced with a steady stream of party-hungry teens, all in search of a golden ticket. I feel like a king, hearing petitions, flanked by my royal advisers (Loch and Co.). I play it cool at Loch's advice, saying numbers are limited, I can only invite a select few. I don't say an absolute no to anyone, and promise to take all requests into consideration.

So I'm a poseur. So sue me.

✠ Just before the bell rings for class, my last petitioner approaches. Bill-E. He's smiling awkwardly, even more so than usual. "Hi, Grubbs."

"Hi."

"How's tricks, Spleenio?" Loch says, putting out his hand. I groan as Bill-E falls for the trick again, makes to shake, and is humiliated when Loch whips his hand away. "Sucker!"

I don't wait for Bill-E or Loch to say anything else. "Have you heard about the party?" I ask quickly.

"Yeah," Bill-E says. "I know I was supposed to come over this weekend, but —"

"You're not going to back out, are you?" I cut him short. "C'mon, Bill-E, this is my first party. I need you there for moral support."

A rosy glow of happiness spreads outwards from the center of the chubby boy's cheeks. "You want me to come?" he asks quietly, half suspecting a cruel joke.

"Of course," I say firmly. "In fact, if you don't, the party's off."

"Now hold on a minute . . ." Loch begins, startled.

"I mean it," I silence him, eyes on Bill-E, trying to put right at least some of the wrong things between us.

"Well . . . I mean . . . I guess . . . OK." Bill-E grins. "Sure. Why not?"

"Great." I raise a warning finger. "But don't tell Ma and Pa Spleen it's a party or they'll never let you come."

"No sheet, Sherlock!" Bill-E laughs and heads off, much happier than I've seen him in a long while.

✠ Dervish is getting ready to leave. In his leather pants and jacket, pulling the straps out of his helmet. His motorcycle's outside the front door, primed to go. "Is the party tonight or tomorrow?" he asks.

"Tomorrow. Too awkward for people to come tonight.

Plus it gives me time to go shopping in the Vale in the morning."

"You know I'll be back early Sunday afternoon," he reminds me.

"I know."

"If I walk in and find pools of puke and mountains of trash . . ."

"You won't," I assure him. "There aren't many coming, and a few are sleeping over, to help clean up in the morning. The only thing is, I'm not sure if I'll be able to do all the laundry before you return."

"That's fine," Dervish says, then raises an eyebrow. "Those staying over are all boys, I presume?"

"Of course."

"They'd better be. Because if I find out otherwise . . ."

"You won't."

"Good."

The pair of massive front doors are already open. Dervish walks out, breathing in fresh spring air. "It's supposed to be cold over the weekend," he says. "Don't leave the windows open or the house will be freezing."

"I have everything under control," I tell him.

"I doubt it." He climbs onto his bike.

"Say hi to Meera for me."

"Sure."

"Give her a kiss for me too."

"Funny guy." Then, without a goodbye, he's off, tearing down the driveway, already approaching the speed limit — and he's only warming up. If everyone drove like my maniac of an uncle, the roads would be awash with blood.

✠ ✠ ✠

✠ This isn't the first time Dervish has left me alone in the house, but it's the first time he's left me in total control. Before, the understanding was always that I was simply holding the fort. No parties. This time he's as good as said the house is mine for the next forty-odd hours, to do whatever I want with it.

It feels strange. I find myself thinking of everything that could go wrong — broken windows, smashed vases, someone stumbling into Dervish's study and turning into a frog. I half wish I could cancel. I've been to a couple of wild parties with Loch over the past few months and never worried about what we were doing, the mess we were making, what would happen to the kids who lived there when their parents returned. Now that the shoe's on my foot, I realize what a risky undertaking it is. Maybe I should fake sick and call the whole thing off.

The phone rings. Loch. It's as if he sensed my wavering mood and intervened to sway me back into party mode. "Has Dervish gone?" he asks.

"Yes."

"Good. I didn't want to discuss it at school — too many ears — but what about booze? Yea or nay?"

"That might be a bit much," I mutter. "Things will probably be wild enough if everyone's sober."

"Yeah, it'll be wilder if everyone's drunk," Loch laughs, "but a lot more fun! I was thinking about all those bottles of wine in the cellar . . ."

"No way," I snap. "Most are expensive. *Very* expensive.

Nobody goes near the wine. That's a golden rule. If anyone breaks it, I'll kick you all out."

"Spoilsport," Loch grumbles. "Well, what about beer? I could ask one of my older cousins to get us a crate or two."

"I'd rather you didn't."

"You're not wimping out, are you?" he asks suspiciously.

"Well . . ." I start.

"Good," Loch says quickly. "Let's forget about the booze then. If anybody brings some, great. If not, we'll manage sober. Fair enough?"

"Yeah," I say unhappily. "I guess."

"Great. See you in the morning. Oh, and I'll be bringing Reni, to help carry the bags. Is that OK?"

"Sure," I say, spirits lifting, instantly forgetting about my reservations. "That'll be . . . fine. Yeah. Whatever."

A short laugh, then Loch hangs up, leaving me to get on with planning the party.

✢ Loch, Reni, and I make three runs to the village. Frank and Leon join us on the last run, when we realize we need more hands. It's brilliant spending so much time with Reni, walking beside her in and out of Carcery Vale, discussing the party, bands, politics . . . whatever she feels like talking about.

Loch offers to chip in some money for the drinks and food, but I tell him it's OK. Dervish is rich — there's a family fortune knocking around, which will one day be mine and Bill-E's — and he never begrudges me anything. He left a wad of cash for me in his study and told me to use it well.

Reni does a lot of the organizing. I spent a couple of hours last night drawing up a list of everything we might need, and was more than a little pleased with myself. She took one look at the list this morning, laughed, and tore it up. "Is Jesus coming?" she asked.

"Uh . . . no," I replied, astonished.

"Then forget about the loaves and fishes miracle. What you had on that list wouldn't last until nine o'clock. Now, grab me a fresh pad and pen — this needs a woman's touch."

Much as I hate to admit it, she was right. Carrying the supplies back from Carcery Vale, it feels like we've bought way too much — we could feed the starving millions with all this. But by the time we've divided it out into plates and bowls and distributed them around the three main party rooms — two big living rooms and the kitchen — it doesn't look like a whole lot.

"Maybe we need to make another run," Frank muses, opening a bag of chips.

"Maybe you need to stop snacking before anyone arrives," Reni retorts, grabbing the bag from him. "No," she says, casting a professional eye around. "This will do. Any more would be a waste." She checks her watch. "I'm going home to get ready. And you boys . . ." She wrinkles her nose and pulls a face. "Ever heard of showers?"

She leaves. I look around at Loch, Frank, and Leon. They stare back. Then we all raise an arm and sniff.

PARTY ANIMAL

✠ ✠ ✠

THE party's not set to start until seven, but the first guests begin arriving right after six. I'm nervous and twitchy, worrying about where their coats should go, if there's enough food and drink, if anyone's smuggled in anything they shouldn't have. But as more arrive and the laughter and buzz of voices increase, I begin to relax as I realize people are having fun.

Not everyone who comes was on the invitation list, but there's nothing I can do about that. If I turned them away, I'd ruin the atmosphere. A few gate-crashers have to be expected at any party.

Loch and Frank help (Leon can't make it until nine), opening the front doors and greeting newcomers while I'm showing others around the mansion. It's cool to be a guide to so many fascinated guests. I love leading them through the halls, pointing out weapons on the walls, explaining the house's bloody history, showing them the hall of portraits and the faces of the dead.

"How come there are so many young people?" Mary asks, studying the paintings and photos.

"We're an adventurous bunch," I lie. "We don't sit around quietly, waiting to grow old. We embrace life and danger, and so a lot of us die young."

"They leave good-looking corpses though," Reni says, and giggles sweetly when I blush.

✠ Bill-E arrives at a quarter to eight. I'm coming down the stairs when he enters, admitted by Loch.

"Hey, Bill-E, great to see you, glad you could come," Loch enthuses, offering his hand, which Bill-E predictably — and, I must admit, amusingly — tries to shake. "Sucker!"

But even Loch's teasing can't spoil the mood. Bill-E breezes past him, feathers only mildly ruffled, and makes for the nearest pile of food. Ten minutes of solid scarfing later, he's by my side, marching after me as I lead the latest group on a tour. Halfway through, he's taken over — he knows much more about the house and its legends than I do and is better at telling the stories. I don't mind. It's nice to see him come out of his shell. I wish he was like this all the time.

✠ As the night ticks on I start to feel strange. Nauseous, dizzy, the rooms and people around me appearing weirdly out of focus. My breath is heavy in my ears and my stomach and chest ache if I move quickly. It's not alcohol — nobody brought booze — but maybe somebody spiked the soft drinks with a spoon of a nasty powder or a pill.

"Are you OK?" Reni asks, spotting me staggering towards the kitchen.

"A bit . . . weird . . ." I gasp, having to sit on the floor a couple of yards shy of the kitchen door.

Reni squats beside me. "You don't look good," she says, and feels my forehead. "You haven't been drinking, have you?" I shake my head. "Drugs?" Her voice is hard.

"Not . . . that I know . . . about," I wheeze. "I was go-ing . . . to the kitchen . . . to check. Think somebody . . . might have spiked . . . the drinks."

"They'd better not," Reni growls, surging to her feet. "I'll have them arrested if they did! You wait here." She storms off to investigate. Five or ten minutes later — hard to keep track of time, my head's throbbing so much — she returns, calmer. "Everyone else is fine. I don't think the drinks have been spiked."

"Maybe I'm just sick," I mutter.

"That's what it looks like," she says, then grabs my arms and hauls me to my feet. "Let's get you outside. Fresh air will do you a world of good."

She steers me through the kitchen and out the back door, then props me against the wall and stands watch beside me as I take deep breaths and try to focus. After a few minutes my head clears a little and my stomach settles.

"Better?" Reni asks, tilting my chin up, examining my eyes.

"Good as new," I smile.

Reni leans towards me, a serious look in her eyes. I tense. Will this be our first kiss? I hope I don't mess up. How do they do it in the movies — tongue or just lips? But at the last moment her expression crinkles and she kisses me quickly on the nose instead of the mouth.

"Come on, Romeo," she laughs, taking my hands. "It's too cold out here for monkey business."

"What about inside?" I murmur, smiling at myself for getting the line out without stammering.

"Maybe later." Reni grins and heads back in. I follow in high spirits, feeling much better than I did a few minutes ago. It's only when we reach the kitchen door that I stop and feel a stab of real panic.

The light's off in the kitchen. I can see the reflection of the sky in the dark glass of the door. Letting go of Reni's hand, turning slowly, I look up at the cloudless heavens and fix my sight on the moon — which is round and fat, dangerously near to full.

✤ Locked inside Dervish's study. Breath coming quickly, raggedly. Trembling wildly. Remembering the night Bill-E changed, the beast he became. Dervish had to cage him up to protect people from him. He would have killed otherwise.

Am I turning into a werewolf?

I don't know. The sickness and dizziness are still there, but they might be more a product of fear than anything else. Maybe it's just worry that's turned me white as a ghost and left me ready to throw up, shaking like a human maraca.

I focus on my hands, willing them steady. After a while they obey me. Then I force myself to breathe normally, evenly. When I feel like I'm in control, I study my reflection in a small hand mirror, looking for telltale signs around the eyes and lips — that's where the marks show first.

Nothing. The same lines and creases. Eyes a bit wilder than normal — which is understandable — but mine. Not clouded over or animalistic.

I wish Dervish was here. I consider calling his cell. He isn't that far away. At the speed he drives, he could be here in a couple of hours. I dig my phone out of my pocket, scroll down to his number, start to bring my thumb down over the dial button . . . then stop.

"I'm not turning," I grunt, angry at myself for being so scared. "It's after ten." I check my watch. "Hell, nearly eleven. The moon's at the height of its powers. If I was going to change, it would have happened by now."

But maybe it's the start, a voice within me whispers, a voice I last heard in *Slawter* many months earlier — the voice of magic. *Nobody changes overnight. It's a gradual process, spread out over a few months. This could be the beginning of the end.*

"Maybe," I agree, refusing to panic. "But I'm not going to turn savage tonight. Nobody has anything to fear from me. So there's no point dragging Dervish back."

But if it's the change . . . If your time as a human is limited . . .

"All the more reason to party hard while I can." I laugh viciously, then make myself go downstairs, smile, and act like everybody else — normal.

Midnight comes and goes. So do most of the guests, walking or biking home, a few collected by their parents. By half past, only those who are sleeping over remain — Loch, Frank, Leon, Charlie, Robbie, Bill-E, Reni, Mary, and a few others who've begged to spend the night. (OK, I lied to Dervish about only boys staying, but what he doesn't know can't hurt him, right?)

"Do you want me to show you where you'll be sleeping?" I ask, eager to wind the party down, still feeling sick.

"The hell with sleep," Frank laughs. "Time for spin the bottle!"

While there are good-natured groans, nobody objects, so five minutes later we're all in the largest of the party rooms, sitting in a nervous circle around an empty bottle. Lots of giggles, nervous looks, licking of lips. I do a quick head count — nine boys, four girls.

"How are we going to work this?" I ask Frank.

"We each take a turn spinning," he says, rubbing his hands together eagerly. "When it points to a member of the opposite sex — *booyah!*"

"But there's more of us than them," I object.

"So?" he frowns.

"Well . . . I mean . . . at least two of them are going to have to kiss more than one guy." Worried about Reni kissing anyone other than me.

Frank laughs. "That's how it works, moron. We all get plenty of action."

"Only simple kisses," Mary interjects. "No groping or tongues, not unless both want to. Clear?"

"Of course, of course!" Frank says quickly, leering.

"We mean it," Reni says. "If one of you breaks the rules, that's it, end of game, you all miss out."

"OK." Frank sighs, rolling his eyes. "We get the message. Now, who first?"

"It's Grubbs's party," Loch says.

"That's OK," I cough, getting cold feet. "I think Bill-E should have first shot."

"I second the motion." Bill-E laughs, more at ease than I've seen him in a long time. He grabs the bottle and spins it madly. It turns . . . turns . . . turns . . . like it's never going to stop. But finally it does — and it's pointing at Reni.

Bill-E grins. "Sorry, amigo, but the bottle decides."

I feel my temper rise as Bill-E and Reni meet in the middle of the circle to a series of whistles and crude remarks. The bile that's been threatening to bubble over all night forces its way up my throat. But then Reni pecks him on the lips and they both sit down. I relax, swallow the vomit, and grin greenly.

The game continues. Great laughs when one of the boys spins and it ends up pointing to another boy. Lewd giggles when that happens to the girls. Most of the kisses are like the first, quick pecks. But a few are stronger, where the pair are attracted to each other — Robbie and Mary, Leon and Nina Duffy.

I get to kiss Mary twice, Nina three times ("This is getting serious," she says jokingly), before Reni finally spins and the bottle ends up pointing at me.

"Whoo-hoo!" Frank chortles.

"Touchdown!" Charlie cries.

"Easy, tiger," Loch grunts, smiling tightly.

Reni and I stand and walk towards each other. Reni nudges the bottle out of the way with her left foot. We smile shakily. Then kiss.

Her lips are drier than I thought they'd be, but nice. My

hands slide around her back and I lock my fingers together, careful not to hug too hard in case I crack her ribs. The kiss continues. Her lips move and mine follow — this is easier than I imagined. I don't know why I was so nervous before. I could get used to this very quickly!

Lots of cheers and whistles. I drown them out, eyes closed, feeling so happy I could burst. A warm fire grows within me, burning away the feeling of sickness, spreading rapidly through my body, squeezing out of my pores like steam. I lose myself in the hot, hypnotic kiss, unaware of anything else.

Then gasps of amazement wreck the moment.

"What the —?"

"How the hell —?"

"Oh, my god!"

My right eye opens an angry fraction — what's everybody getting so worked up about? Then I spot it. The bottle, spinning again, but not on the ground — a few feet above the floor, suspended in midair, floating upwards as it spins.

The bottle rises smoothly. Everyone (with a single exception) is on their feet, backing away, alarmed. Reni realizes something's wrong. She breaks off the kiss, takes a step back, sees the bottle. Her expression freezes.

Bill-E's the only one not moving. He's staring at the bottle intently. I think for a second that he's controlling it, using one of Dervish's spells. I huff myself up to roar at him. But then I catch the alarm in his eyes and realize he's trying to stop it. *I'm* the one making it rise.

The bottle reaches a point about two feet above my head,

then levels out. It's spinning faster now, making a small whirring sound.

"What's happening?" Robbie shouts. "Grubbs, are you doing this?"

I don't answer. My gaze is on the bottle. Although it's spinning too quickly for the eye to follow, I find that I can slow the action down. The world seems to go into slow motion around me. People's mouths move infinitely slowly. Words reach me as though dragged through a pipe from a long way away.

"Grrruuuubbbsssss! Whaaaaattttt'sss . . . goooiiiinnnggggg ooonnnnn?"

The bottle explodes, and the world speeds up again. Shards of glass shoot at me, Reni, everybody in the room, at our faces and eyes. Instinctively, I bark a word of magic. I don't know what the word is or where it comes from. But it freezes the shards in place. They hang in midair, dozens of tiny pieces of glass, pointing at us like a flight of mini arrows.

"No way!" somebody shouts, more excited than afraid. My friends start lowering the hands that they'd instinctively raised to protect themselves.

Bill-E stares at the bits of glass, then at me. His eyebrows are furrowed. He knows this is magic but he can't understand how I'm doing it. He saw me do more than this in Slawter, but that enclosed area was crackling with magical energy. Many of us could perform amazing feats there. In the real, normal world, he thought — like Dervish — that I had all the magical ability of a duck.

"Grubbs," Reni says uncertainly, touching my right elbow. "Are you OK?"

"Yes," I whisper.

"Do you know what's happening?" Scared, looking for re-assurance, gazing at the shard nearest her face, worried it might shoot forward again.

"Yes," I smile. Without knowing how I'm doing any of this, I wave a hand at the glass and several pieces turn into flower petals, which drop slowly, beautifully, to the floor. I wave my other hand and more shards turn into butterflies. They fly away, zoning in on the light overhead. One last wave and the rest of the glass is transformed, a mixture of butter-flies and flowers.

I grab one of the falling petals and present it to Reni. "For you, my lady."

Then everybody's cheering, patting my back, grabbing for petals and butterflies, demanding to know how the trick was performed.

Only Bill-E knows there was no trick. Only he realizes this was real magic. And only he can possibly understand and share in my sense of bewilderment and gut-stabbing fear.

✠ Later. Everyone but Bill-E and me has gone to bed. I'm at the door of my room, still holding a petal. Bill-E's facing me, eyes steady and serious. "How'd you do it?"

"Dervish has been teaching me."

Bill-E shakes his head. "Bull. Dervish told me you don't want to learn magic. He's cool with that. But even if he *was* teaching you, that's way beyond anything I've ever seen him do. Apart from in *Slawter*." He looks around nervously. "Are demons breaking through? Did you tap into their power?"

"No. We're safe here. Demons can't cross in Carcery Vale."

"Then how did you do it?" he presses. "Where did the magic come from?"

I shake my head miserably. "Forget about it. This doesn't concern you."

"I might be able to help if I —"

"I told you it's none of your business!" Bill-E looks hurt, and I feel sorry immediately. "It's no big deal," I lie. "This has been building up for a long time. I haven't spoken with Dervish about it, but after tonight I guess I'll have to."

"This isn't the first time it's happened?" Bill-E asks.

"There have been signs, but nothing this obvious."

"Do you think . . ." He can hardly bring himself to say it. "Do you think you might be a magician?"

"No. Dervish would know if I was. But maybe I've got more potential than we thought. I might be a latent mage. If so, Dervish will know what to do."

Bill-E nods, starts to leave, looks back. "You won't be able to turn away from it anymore," he says softly. "Magic, I mean. You'll have to learn now, so you can control it. If you hadn't been able to stop that glass tonight . . . if you hadn't turned it into butterflies and flowers . . ."

"I know," I sigh.

"You'll really tell Dervish? You won't try to keep it a secret?"

"I'll tell him. I'm not a fool. I know what magic can do if it isn't properly channeled. I don't want to hurt anyone."

Bill-E smiles, says good night, and leaves.

I slip into my bedroom, lie on top of the covers fully

clothed, and stare at the ceiling, listening to my heart pound and my blood swoosh through my body, trying to make sense of whatever the hell is happening inside me.

✠ Later. Slowly coming awake. Sluggishly realizing I must have fallen asleep on top of the bed. Then I click to the fact I'm not on the bed anymore. I'm standing by the round stained-glass window in my bedroom, listening to howls outside. No, not outside — in here!

My head whips around in panic. Fully awake now. I can't see anything in the room but I can hear the howls of a werewolf! Where is it? It must be close. It's so loud. Where . . . ?

With a jolt, I realize he's in the glass in front of me. At least his reflection is.

My face is darker than it was earlier. A wicked glint to my eyes. Lips pulled back over my teeth. Raising a hand, I see that my fingers are curling inwards, clawlike. I start to howl again, stepping into the colored rays of the moon.

I stop. Focusing on my reflection, I feel the same warmth that I felt when I was kissing Reni, just before the bottle started to rise. I study my face, the sharp lines, the wild eyes. Directing the warmth towards it, I wish the mask away, wanting my normal face back, telling this vision of a manwolf to go.

And it does. Even though it shouldn't, my skin resumes its ordinary shape and color. My lips droop back down over my teeth. My fingers unclench. The howl dies in my throat and becomes a dry cough.

Moments later I'm me again, standing by the window, bathed by the tinted light of a moon which for some reason is no longer affecting me. The warmth is still there. I hold on to it like a security blanket, take it to bed with me, and sustain it, keeping it alive through the rest of the long, weary night, too terrified to close my eyes, afraid of what I might turn into if I drop my guard and give myself over to unprotected sleep.

TREASURE HUNT

✠   ✠   ✠

I sneak a few hours of shut-eye postdawn, when the sun's chased the moon off and I'm safe. But it's an uneasy sleep, filled with nightmares of werewolves and a body in revolt. I imagine myself doing awful things, causing chaos. Only it's not entirely me. It's a beast with my shape and form but with a twisted face, fangs instead of teeth, claws instead of nails, blood-soaked hair.

Grubbs Grady — monster extraordinaire.

✠ When I stumble down the stairs a little after noon, most of the cleaning has been taken care of. Loch tells me Reni had them all up at ten and working like demons. (His choice of wording is unfortunate!) She had to leave at eleven but left him in charge to make sure nobody slacked off.

"That was some trick you pulled," Leon says, sweeping up petals from the living room floor. "I'd love to know how you did it."

"It was magic," Charlie says, shooing a butterfly out through an open window.

"A magic trick," Leon corrects him.

"No, real magic," Charlie insists. "It was, wasn't it, Grubbs? I've seen the books lying around, about wizards, witches, and stuff. It was real magic, right?"

"No." I force a thin smile. "Just a trick. There's no such thing as real magic."

"But the books —" Charlie exclaims.

"— are just books," I finish tiredly, then go to see what state the kitchen's in.

As I'm leaving, I hear Leon mutter, "Magic! You're a real ass sometimes."

"I don't care what he says," Charlie sulks. "I know what I saw. It *was* real magic. I'd bet a million jelly beans on it."

When everything's as clean as we can get it, my friends say goodbye and make their way home to recover before school on Monday. Bill-E and Loch stay — they're going to spend the day here. Bill-E waits till Loch's in the bathroom, then asks how I'm feeling.

"Fine," I lie as my brain throbs with a splitting headache and my stomach gives a sickly rumble.

"I heard howling last night," Bill-E says. "After we'd gone to bed. It woke me. A few others too. There was some talk of it this morning but not much. Most people were still trying to figure out how you pulled off the trick with the bottle."

I grunt, saying nothing.

"Grubbs," Bill-E says hesitantly, "I know we've never discussed the family curse. You filled me in on the basics in Slawter, but you've never offered more information and I haven't pushed."

For a long time Bill-E thought Dervish was the one who'd almost changed into a werewolf. I finally told him the truth in Slawter, only neglecting the part about Dervish being his uncle, not his father. I've never told Bill-E that we share the same Dad. I want to, but he feels a special bond with Dervish, believing him to be his real father. I've never had the heart to burst his bubble.

"Well," Bill-E continues after an uncomfortable pause, "I know I almost turned into a werewolf and that you and Dervish saved me. You faced Lord Loss and won back my humanity. But is the cure definitely permanent?"

"Yes."

"I'm safe? For certain?"

"One hundred percent." I smile.

"What about . . . ?" He hesitates again. "Your magic . . . the howling . . . Are *you* safe too?"

I don't answer for a second. Then, quietly, I lie. "Yes."

"I won't have to lock you up in the cage in the secret cellar?"

"No," I laugh edgily. I hate that cellar. I've only been there once since we defeated Lord Loss, when Dervish's nightmares were threatening to destroy his sanity. "I'm fine. That wasn't me howling. Probably just a big dog that got loose. Now stop worrying — you're getting on my nerves."

Loch returns, wiping his hands dry on his pants, and the questions stop, though I sense Bill-E doesn't fully believe me. He knows something's wrong, that I'm not coming clean. But he doesn't suspect the worst, or anything near it. He trusts me. Thinks of me as his closest friend. Doesn't believe I'd lie point-blank to him about something this serious.

How little he knows.

✤ A long, anticlimactic Sunday. Lounging around the house, all three of us bored, channel surfing in search of something decent to watch, sticking CDs on, turning them off after just a few tracks. Loch makes cutting remarks about Bill-E, winding him up. I worry about lycanthropy and magic.

"This is crap," Loch mutters, switching the TV and CD player to standby. He jumps up and rubs his hands together. "Let's wrestle."

"I'm not in the mood."

"C'mon!" he prods, slapping my face lightly, trying to sting me into action.

"No." I yawn.

Loch scowls, then switches his attention to Bill-E. "How about you, Spleenio?" He grabs the shorter boy by the waist and swings him around.

"Let go!" Bill-E shouts, kicking out.

"We've got a live one," Loch laughs. He throws Bill-E to the ground, then falls on him and starts to tickle.

"No!" Bill-E gasps, face red, slapping at Loch like a girl, half laughing from the tickling, half crying.

"Leave him alone," I mutter angrily — the noise is making my headache worse.

Loch stops and stands. "Sorry, Bill-E," he says. "Let me help you up." He lowers his right hand. Bill-E reaches for it, and Loch whips the hand away. "You're the sultan of suckers, Spleen," he chortles, strolling towards the kitchen, shaking his head with amused disgust.

Bill-E glares daggers at Loch, then at me. "Gossel's scum," he hisses. "I don't care if he is your new best friend. He's the scum of the earth. Shame on you for hanging out with him."

"Don't take it out on me," I snap. "You want to get Loch off your back? Then face him like a man, not a little girl. He bullies you because you let him."

"No, he bullies me because he's a bully," Bill-E retorts, furious tears in his eyes.

I shrug, too exhausted and soreheaded to argue. "Whatever."

Loch returns and Bill-E shuts up, but he glowers like an old man whose pipe's been stolen, then storms off and returns with his coat.

"Going home?" I ask as he buttons it up.

"No," he snarls. "I'm doing what I originally planned to do."

"Huh?"

"You remember. My original plan. If there hadn't been a party." I stare at him blankly and he nods in the direction of the forest.

"Oh," I chuckle. "Lord Sheftree."

"What's that?" Loch asks.

"Nothing," Bill-E says quickly, shooting me a warning look that I ignore, still sore at him for having a go at me. (And sore at myself too, for not being the friend — the brother — he deserves.)

"You know the stories of Lord Sheftree, the guy who used to own this place?" I ask Loch.

"The baby and the piranha, yeah, sure."

"Grubbs . . ." Bill-E growls, not wanting to share our secret with an outsider.

"There's a legend about his treasure." I take grim satisfaction from Bill-E's enraged expression.

"Treasure?" Loch echoes, interested.

"Apparently he had hoards of gold and jewels that nobody ever found. They say he buried it somewhere around here. That it's still sitting there, underground, waiting . . ."

Loch squints at me, then at Bill-E. "This true, Spleenio?"

"Get stuffed."

Loch's face stiffens. "I asked if it was true," he says, taking a menacing step forward.

"Yeah, maybe, so what?" Bill-E squeaks, shrinking away from Loch.

"Any idea where the treasure is?" Loch asks.

"Up your butt," I chip in, and both Loch and Bill-E laugh, the tension vanishing in an instant.

"Nah, come on, really," Loch says, facing me again. "Is this for real or is Spleen-boy paying me back for all those fake handshakes?"

"The legend's real," I tell him. "I don't know about the treasure. We've been all over the forest, dug more holes than a pair of rabbits, and found nothing. Right, Bill-E?"

"Yeah." Bill-E sighs, resigning himself to sharing our secret with Loch. "But you bury treasure because you want it to be hard to find. There wouldn't have been much point in

Lord Sheftree putting it where anyone could find it. It's out there, I'm sure, and one day, if we keep trying . . ." He trails off into silence, eyes distant.

"I thought you were rich anyway," Loch says to me. "Why are you bothered about a pile of buried treasure?"

"I'm not. But it would be exciting if it did exist and we found it. Bill-E and I used to spend a lot of our weekends looking for it. Even though we never found anything, the searching was fun."

"You gave up?" Loch asks.

I shrug. "Bill-E goes looking every so often, but it's been a while since I went with him."

"He's been too busy wrestling with blockheads," Bill-E says bitterly, but Loch ignores the remark.

"I've never searched for treasure," Loch says. "How do you do it — with a metal detector?"

"No," Bill-E says. "We walk around with shovels, looking for likely spots. Then we make trial holes. If nothing turns up, we fill in the holes and move on."

"Sounds amateurish," Loch says dubiously.

Bill-E laughs. "Like *Grubitsch* said, the searching is fun. You'd need expensive equipment to go after it seriously. For us it's always been a game."

"What about it?" Loch asks me.

"You want to go on a treasure hunt?" I groan, wishing I could just go back to bed for a few hours.

"It'd beat sitting around here, doing nothing," Loch says.

"But it's raining," I protest.

"A light drizzle. It'll clear soon. C'mon, it's something different."

"Not for Bill-E and me."

"But it is for *me*," Loch presses.

"Why don't you and Bill-E go by yourselves?" I suggest.

"No way!" they both exclaim at the same time, then look at each other and laugh, temporary (*very* temporary!) allies.

"I'll let him tag along if you come," Bill-E says. "Otherwise I'll go home. I still have some homework to finish."

"C'mon," Loch huffs again. "Don't be such a spoilsport, Grubbs."

"OK," I groan, rising reluctantly. "Give me a few minutes to change. Loch, you and Bill-E go get some shovels. Bill-E knows where to find them."

"Cool!" Loch grins, slapping Bill-E on the back. "You leave it to the Spleenster and me — we know what we're doing."

"Just one thing," Bill-E says stiffly. "On the very off chance that we find any treasure, it's ours. You don't have any rights to it, understand? I don't want you going all *Treasure of the Sierra Madre* on us."

"Treasure of where?" Loch frowns.

"It's a black-and-white movie," Bill-E explains as he leads Loch away. "I'll fill you in on the plot while we're getting the shovels. It's all about treasure hunters and the destructive nature of paranoid greed. . . ."

✠ The fresh air clears my head a little bit, but after an hour of aimless walking and digging I'd still rather be in bed. Loch's loving it though, digging wildly, *accidentally* hitting Bill-E with clumps of dirt every so often to break the monotony. Bill-E doesn't mind too much. He's just glad I'm out scouring the forest with him again, even if we do have an extra (unwanted) passenger in tow.

"We've found a few bits and pieces over the years," Bill-E explains as we give up on our third trial dig and refill the hole. "Old coins, scraps of clothes, half a knife."

"Anything worth money?" Loch asks.

"Not really," Bill-E says. "One of the coins would have been valuable if it had been in better condition, but it was pretty worn and part of it was missing. Dervish let me keep it."

"Why were they buried if they were worthless?" Loch asks.

"They weren't," Bill-E says. "The level of the ground's constantly changing. Things fall or are thrown away. Grass and weeds grow over them. They sink when the ground's wet. New earth blows over them. In no time at all they're a few feet underground . . . a yard . . . more. The world's always burying castoffs and stuff that's been forgotten. Heck, even the giant Sphinx in Egypt was half buried once and almost lost forever."

"No way," Loch snorts.

"It's true," Bill-E says. "We did it in history. And there are loads of important places in Egypt today — burial chambers and the like — that are covered up. In some towns they know where they are, but people have built houses over them, so they can't excavate."

"I never learned any of that in history," Loch says suspiciously.

"Well," Bill-E replies smugly, "maybe if you were in the *advanced* classes . . ."

✤ ✤ ✤

✤ Loch's starting to tire of the wandering and digging. I'm glad. Aside from the fact that I'm weary and grumpy, it's late afternoon and it won't be much longer before the sun starts to set and an even fuller moon than last night's rises over the earth like a plum dipped in cream. Maybe Dervish is back already. If so, I want to sit down with him and have a long talk about what's going on in my life and what we need to do about it.

"This sucks," Loch grumbles, studying his hand where he cut it on the last hole.

"One more try," Bill-E says. "We'll quit after that."

"Why not now?" Loch says. "This is stupid. We'll never find anything."

"It's an old superstition of ours. When we decide we've had enough, we always dig one last hole. Right, Grubbs?"

"Yeah," I mutter. "That's the way we've always done it."

"And look where it got you." Loch snorts but goes along with the plan, not wanting to be the one who quits first.

Bill-E leads us farther into the wild bushes of the forest, trying to pick a good spot for the final dig of the day. Briars catch on my pants and jacket, and one scratches deep into my neck, drawing a few drops of blood and a loud curse. I'm about to call an end to the farce and demand we go home immediately, regardless of superstitions, when something about the landscape makes me pause.

We're in the middle of a thicket, lots of natural weeds and bushes. It looks much the same as any other part of the forest to the untrained eye, but when you've spent a few years exploring a particular area, you see things differently. You get to know the various types of trees, flowers, and weeds.

You make mental pointers so you can find your way around easily and quickly. I've been here before, I'm sure of it, but I can't remember when. . . .

The memory clicks into place. It was shortly before Bill-E turned into a werewolf, before Dervish told me about the Demonata and Lord Loss. Bill-E and I were on one of our treasure hunts. We'd started to dig around here when Bill-E spotted Dervish and went all mysterious. He made me hide, so Dervish didn't see us, then we followed him. That was the day Bill-E hit me with his theory about werewolves. The day my destiny fell into place and I started on a collision course with Lord Loss and his vile familiars.

"Let's dig here."

"I'm not sure." Bill-E frowns, studying the ground. "The earth looks hard."

"No," I say, casting around. "There's a soft spot somewhere, between a couple of stones. At least there used to be . . ."

I find it and give a grunt of satisfaction. I can still see faint marks from where I began to dig last time, a minute or so before Bill-E went weird on me and the world of werewolves claimed me for its own.

"How'd you know that was there?" Bill-E asks.

"Magic," I reply with a laugh, then drive my shovel into the soil.

Half an hour later, nobody's laughing. We're surrounded by three fresh mounds of dirt and stones, digging deeper by the minute, cutting down at an angle. There's a large rock buried just beneath the briars and grass, under the shelter of which the dirt and stones lie. There's rock to either side too. It's too early to tell for certain, but this looks like the entrance to a tunnel or cave.

"What's that?" Loch says suddenly, stooping. He comes up holding something golden. My heart leaps. Bill-E and I crowd around him, muttering with excitement. Then he holds it up to the dim light and we see it's just an orangey-yellow stone. "Damn!" Loch hurls it away.

Bill-E makes a face and keeps digging. He's working on the sides, clearing the rock faces, while Loch and I dig straight down. Bill-E pauses after a while and strokes the rock. "Hard to tell if this fissure is natural or man-made. The sides are smooth, as if they'd been ground down. But I guess they'd feel just as smooth if nature had done the grinding."

Loch hits a larger stone and winces. Scrapes around it to find its edges, then inserts the tip of his shovel under one corner and tells me to help him. Together we lever it out, then lift it up onto the bank around us. We're knee-high in the hole (based on my long legs, not Bill-E's stumpy pins) by this stage.

Loch clears the gap left by the stone, then scowls. "There's another one. Looks even bigger than the first."

"It's getting rockier the farther down we dig," I note.

"That's logical," Bill-E says. "The heavier stones sink deeper than the smaller ones."

"Is it worth carrying on?" Loch asks. "I don't think there's any treasure here."

"How do you figure that?" Bill-E sneers.

"Makes sense," Loch says. "This Lord Sheftree miser would have wanted easy access to his treasure, so he could dig it up whenever he liked. This ground's too rocky. Too much hard work. It would have been easier for him to do it somewhere else."

"Hey," Bill-E says, "this is a maniac we're talking about — the guy fed a baby to his piranha! Who knows what he might or might not have done? Maybe he hired men to dig this hole, then killed them and left them to rot with the treasure. Maybe he had others dig it up every few years, so he could put more treasure down there, then killed them too. Heck, there could be dozens of skeletons down there."

Loch and I share an uneasy glance.

"I don't know if I want to go digging up skeletons," Loch mumbles.

"Afraid of a few old bones, *Gosselio?*" Bill-E cackles.

"No. But if there are corpses, we shouldn't disturb their remains."

"Not even if they're sitting on a chest of gold coins?" Bill-E taunts him. "Five chests? Ten? Not even if we agree to cut you in on a slice of the profits?"

"A while ago you said there was nothing in it for me," Loch snaps.

"You can't expect an equal share," Bill-E drawls, "but if there's a fortune and you help us dig it up, we'll take care of you. Won't we, Grubbs?"

"Too much talking," I grunt, stabbing my shovel into the ground, trying to find a crack I can use to pry out the next big stone. "Dig."

✠ ✠ ✠

✠ Almost sunset. Without discussing it, we come to a halt and study the fruits of our labor. The hole is thigh-deep now. It's been hard going for the past twenty minutes — one big, awkward stone after another. At least the hole's no wider than when we started, so we've only got to worry about digging down, not out to the sides as well.

"We could be at this forever." Loch gasps, wiping sweat from his forehead. All three of us are sweating badly. "No telling how deep it goes."

"What do you say, Bill-E?" I ask, glancing up at the setting sun, feeling the sickness and headache building within me again. "Time to stop?"

"Yeah," Bill-E agrees. "We can't dig in the dark. But we'll come back, right?" He looks at me, Loch, then me again. "We could be on to the find of the millennium. Feet — maybe inches — away from Lord Sheftree's treasure. We can't walk away from that."

"He's right," Loch says. "It's probably just a big old hole, but . . ."

"What about next weekend?" I suggest.

"I can't wait that long," Bill-E says. "A whole week thinking about it, dreaming of the treasure . . ."

"Also, what if somebody else comes by, sees the hole, and finishes what we've started?" Loch growls. "There aren't any fences around your land, are there?"

"No." I clear my throat. "Actually, this isn't *our* land. We don't own this part of the forest."

Loch stares at me hard, then at Bill-E, who fidgets uncomfortably. "You don't have legal rights to it?" he says softly. "You were bluffing, trying to cut me out of any find."

Bill-E shrugs. "You wouldn't have known about the treasure if we hadn't told you. Anyway, it's ours — Grubbs's — by right of birth."

"No, it's not," Loch objects. "He isn't any relation to Lord Sheftree. Dervish just bought the house, that's all. If I wanted, I could come back here with others and dig without you."

Bill-E gulps and looks to me for help.

"Thirds," I say steadily. "An equal split. Assuming there's anything down there. And assuming we get to keep it if there is. For all we know, there are laws that won't allow us to keep any of it. But if the treasure's there and we can make a claim, we divide it in three. Agreed?"

"Agreed," Loch says quickly.

Bill-E looks disgusted but nods angrily. "OK."

"And we don't tell anybody, not until we figure out what our rights are," Loch adds. "There's no point doing all the hard work and not being able to reap the rewards. If we find treasure, we keep our mouths shut and check the law. We might have to wait till we're eighteen to declare our find. Or maybe we can never declare it. Maybe we'll have to sell it on the black market." He grins. "The gold and diamond market!"

"I'm not so sure about that," Bill-E says. "Not revealing a find like this could land us in a lot of trouble."

"We can buy our way out of it with the money we make from the treasure." Loch laughs. "Either way, we don't say anything until we know, right?" Bill-E and I share a glance, then nod. "Great. It's settled." He hauls himself out of the hole and lays his shovel aside. "I don't know about you two, but I plan to be back here first thing after school tomorrow, and every day this week, and the week after, and the week after that, until we get to the bottom of this damn hole. You with me?"

"I'll come," Bill-E agrees. "Not every day — Gran and Grandad would get suspicious if I was late coming home every evening — but most of the time it shouldn't be a problem."

"Grubbs?" Loch asks.

"I'll be here," I promise, glad to have something to distract me from my recent fears. I look up at the darkening sky and add a proviso. "But only until dusk. I'm not staying out here nights. Not when the moon's up."

✤ Home. Waiting for Dervish. He should have returned by now. I call his cell, to check that everything's OK, but only get his voice mail. Sitting in the TV room, TV switched off, no lights on. In my guts and bones I can feel the moon rising. Concentrating on my breathing, willing myself not to change, trying to stay human.

✤ Without any sound of a motorcycle, the doors open at about ten o'clock and Dervish stumbles in. "My head," he groans, slumping on the couch next to me, a hand thrown over his eyes.

"What's wrong?" I ask, thinking he's been in a crash. Then I catch the stench of alcohol. "You're drunk!"

"I forgot how much Meera can drink when she puts her mind to it," he mumbles. "And unlike normal people, she doesn't get a hangover the next morning. She was at it again first thing when she got up, and she made me join in." He puts his hands over his ears and moans. "The bells, the bells!"

"Tell me you didn't drive home in this state," I snap.

"You think I'm crazy?" Dervish huffs. "I cast a sobering spell."

"You're full of it!"

"No, really, it works perfectly. Except it's very short-term. It ran out when I got near Carcery Vale. I had to stop and walk the rest of the way. And the worst thing is, when it wears off, the hangover kicks in with twice as much venom as before." Dervish doubles over, head cradled between his hands, whining like a kicked dog.

"Serves you right," I sniff. "You should have more sense at your age."

"Please, Grubbs, don't play mother," Dervish groans. He staggers to his feet and heads for the kitchen. "I'm going to make an absolutely huge cup of hot chocolate, then retire to my room for the night. I don't want to be disturbed unless the house is burning." He pauses. "Strike that. I don't want to be disturbed even then. Let me burn — I'd be better off."

I think about calling him back, making him sit down and listen to me. But it wouldn't be fair. Better to let him get a good night's sleep, then tell him about it tomorrow. Besides, I don't feel too sick at the moment, not as bad as I felt last night. I don't want to jinx myself, but I think I might be over the worst.

✠ ✠ ✠

✠ Dervish's snores rock the house to its foundations. I don't want to sleep. I want to keep a vigil, stay focused on my breathing, alert to any hint of a change. But I'm exhausted. All the energy that went into the party . . . lack of sleep last night . . . walking and digging this afternoon. My eyelids refuse to stay open. Even coffee — which I hardly ever drink — doesn't work.

I undress and slip into a T-shirt and boxers. Slide beneath the covers. Lying there, I think that maybe I should get a rope, tie it round my ankles and the bed frame, maybe tie up one of my hands too. That should hold me in case I change during the night. A good plan, but it comes too late. Even as I'm gearing myself up to get out of bed and fetch a rope, my eyelids slam down and I'm out for the count.

✠ Harsh breathing. Thumping sounds. Cold night air.

I come to my senses slowly, the same as last night. I see a pair of hands lifting a large rock out of the ground. They throw it overhead casually as if it were a pebble. They stoop, start clearing more dirt away . . . then stop as I realize they're *my* hands. I exert my will and look around.

I'm standing in a hole, dressed only in my T-shirt and boxers. Bare feet. Dirt-encrusted fingers. It takes me a few seconds to realize I'm in the hole where we were digging earlier. The reason I didn't recognize it instantly — it's about four times deeper than when we left it.

I look up. I'm about six feet below ground level, surrounded by rock. In a sudden panic, afraid the rocks are going to grind together and crush me, I grab a handhold and haul myself up. A couple of quick thrusts later, I'm standing by the edge of the hole, shivering from cold and fear, looking around with wonder.

There are rocks and dirt everywhere. I don't know how long I was down there, but I must have been digging like a madman. The weird thing is, I don't feel the least bit tired. My muscles aren't aching. Apart from some scared gasping, my breath comes normally and my heart beats as regularly as if I'd been out for a gentle stroll.

I walk over to one of the biggest stones. Study it silently, warily. I bend, grab it by the sides, give an exploratory lift. I can shift it a few inches and that's it, I have to drop it. It weighs a freaking ton. Under any normal circumstances I doubt I could lift it higher than knee level, not without throwing my back out completely. Yet I must have. And not only picked it up, but lobbed it out of the hole too.

Back to the rim of the mini abyss. Staring down into darkness. What brought me here? I'd like to think I was just sleepwalking, that I came here because I'd been thinking about the hole all evening. But there's more to it than that. My senses are on high alert, animal sharp (*wolf* sharp), and I don't think it's any accident that I wound up here, digging as if my life depended on it.

As much as I don't want to, I sit, turn, and lower myself into the hole. When I'm at the bottom, I allow a few seconds for my eyes to adjust, then take a really good look. The hole isn't any wider than it was earlier. The rocks on the sides run down smoothly, like a mine shaft. The angle that we were following has continued, so although it's a steep slope, it's easy to climb up and down.

I bend and touch the next rock in line for removal. It's jammed firmly in the earth. I tug hard and it barely moves. Yet I'm sure, if I'd tried a few minutes ago, while asleep, I could have ripped it out and . . .

Whispers.

I frown and cock my head. The sound has been there for a while, maybe since I regained my senses, but I thought it was the wind in the trees. Now that I focus, I realize it's not coming from the trees. It seems to be coming from the rocks.

A bolt of excitement cuts through my confusion and apprehension. Maybe I'm close to a cave and the noise is the wind whistling between earth and rock. I flash on an image of Lord Sheftree's treasure and the glory of being the first to discover it. With renewed enthusiasm I grasp the rock again and pull as hard as I can. I might not be able to toss it out of the hole, but if I can budge it slightly, maybe I can . . .

A flicker on the rock. A slight bulging. A shadow grows out of it, just for a second, then disappears.

I fall backwards, stifling a scream, heart racing.

Eyes fixed to the rock, waiting for it to change again. A minute passes. Two.

I get to my feet, legs *very* shaky, and climb out of the hole, not looking back. I make for home quickly, head down, striding through the forest, ignoring the twigs, stones, and thorns that jab at my bare feet.

Trying hard not to think about what I saw (or thought I

saw). But I can't block it out. It keeps coming back, rattling round the inside of my skull like a rabid rat in a cage.

The flicker . . . the bulging . . . the shadow . . .

It might have been a trick of the light or my skittish mind, but it looked to me like a face was trying to force its way up through the rock from the other side. A human face. A *girl's.*

HARD WORK

✠ ✠ ✠

No sign of Dervish in the morning. He's normally an early riser, so I guess he's still suffering from his binge drinking this weekend. I want to wake him, tell him about my inner turmoil, the magic, the howling, what happened at the hole. But instead I decide to let him sleep in and get his head together. We'll discuss it when I come home after school, when he can think and focus clearly.

Scrubbing hard in the bathroom. The dirt doesn't want to come off. Especially bad under my nails. Without wanting to, I think about grave diggers — their hands must be stained like this all the time.

Looking up when I've scraped them as clean as I can. My reflection in the mirror. Remembering the face I saw/ imagined in the rock. Something about it bugs me. It's not just the fact that there shouldn't have been a face in the rock at all. There's something more . . . something else. . . .

I'm on my way out the front door when it strikes me. The face looked ever so slightly like my dead sister, Gret.

✠ ✠ ✠

✠ The day passes slowly, as if I'm experiencing it second-hand, watching somebody else's body going through the motions of a normal school day. Talking with Charlie, Leon, and Shannon. Greeting Reni with a big smile when she arrives with Loch. Making light of my friends' compliments about the party. Shrugging off the incident with the bottle — "A good magician never reveals his secrets."

Bill-E turns up. I know he's itching to discuss the cave with Loch and me, but we can't speak of it in front of the others, so he slides past silently. Loch yells an insult after him, meaner than usual, maybe to cover up the fact that he's become Bill-E's secret ally.

Classes don't interest me. The teachers could be ghosts for all the impression they make. Fading in and out of conversations between classes and at lunch. The major part of my mind stuck on the twists of the last few nights, the hole I've dug, the face in the rock, the beast I'm apparently becoming.

✠ Heading back to class after the lunch bell. Loch and I are by ourselves. Bill-E hurries up to us and says quietly, "Still on for after school?"

"Sure," Loch says.

"No." Both stare at me. "Dervish wants me home," I lie. "Not sure what it's about. Maybe something valuable got smashed at the party."

Loch winces. "Bad luck. Guess it's just me and Spleenio then." He pinches Bill-E's cheek.

"Get off!" Bill-E yelps, pulling away, rubbing his cheek. "That hurt."

"Sue me," Loch laughs.

Bill-E turns his back on him. "Maybe you can come later?" he asks me.

"I doubt it." I sigh.

Bill-E looks worried. "Perhaps I'll cancel too, leave it till tomorrow."

"No, you don't," Loch grunts. "If you back out now, you stay out. This is a joint venture. If you don't pull your weight — and I know that's a heavy load to pull, you chubby little freak — get lost. We don't need free riders."

Bill-E's fists ball up. The rage inside him froths to the surface. I think he's finally going to go for Loch and I silently will him on. If he fights back, maybe that will be the end of the teasing and Loch will start treating Bill-E as an equal.

But then Bill-E looks Loch over, sizes up his height and muscles, and chickens out. His hands go limp and he turns away with a weak, "See you later then."

Loch leans over and mock-whispers to me, just loud enough for Bill-E to hear, "Do you think anyone would notice if I took Spleeny out to that hole and made him *disappear?*"

"Shut up, you jerk," I snap, and march ahead of him, paying no attention to his theatrical gasp.

✠ Home. No Dervish. A note on the kitchen table. "Went to get my bike. Don't worry about fixing me dinner — still not in the mood for solids."

Damn it! Of all the times in my life, why does Dervish

pick these few days to be Mr. Impossible to Pin Down! Now I wish I'd hit him with the news as soon as he got home. Would have served the old souse right.

Too itchy-footed to wait for him. Better to do something than hang around here, struggling to kill time with homework and TV. So a quick change of clothes, a hasty sandwich, then it's off to the hole to find out what Loch and Bill-E make of my late-night digging marathon.

✠ They're baffled. Standing around the pit when I arrive, jaws slack, staring from the rocks and piles of dirt down into the hole, then back again. Both are holding shovels limply and look like you could knock them over with a fart.

"Hell," I gasp playfully. "You've been working hard."

"We didn't do it," Loch says numbly.

"It was like this when we arrived," Bill-E mutters.

I force a frown. "What are you talking about?"

"We haven't been digging," Loch says, becoming animated. "We only got here a few minutes ago. We found it like this."

"But who . . . how . . . what the heck?" Bill-E mumbles.

We spend ten minutes debating the *mystery*. The simplest solution, which I offer shamelessly, is that somebody discovered the hole after we'd left and did some digging themselves. Bill-E and Loch dismiss it instantly — there are no shovel marks in the newly excavated sections, and no footprints except our own. (I didn't leave any barefooted prints in the night. I must have been extra light on my feet. Padded softly . . . like a wolf.) Besides, they argue, who the hell would go digging in the middle of the night?

"An earthquake?" I suggest as an alternative.

Snorts of derision. We don't get earthquakes here. Besides, even if we did, that wouldn't explain the dirt and rocks piled up around the hole.

Loch wonders if a wild animal is responsible.

"What sort of animal do you think that might be?" Bill-E sneers. "A troll or an ogre? Or maybe it was elves, like in the fairy tale with the shoemaker."

Eventually Bill-E comes up with a theory that satisfies all three of us, at least in the absence of anything more believable. "Lord Sheftree," he says. "If this is where his treasure's buried, maybe he booby-trapped the entrance with explosives. When we were digging, we set them off, but because they'd been buried so long, they didn't ignite right away. It took them a few hours to explode, by which time we were safely home, clear of the blast radius."

"I dunno," Loch mutters, examining the rocks around us. "These look like they were pulled out cleanly, not blasted."

"Maybe it was a catapult-type mechanism," Bill-E says, warming to his theory. "He had all these rocks loaded on a platform, which was set to shoot them upwards when the trap was sprung. They'd crush anyone nearby."

We discuss it further, trying to figure how the trap worked and wondering if there might be more than just one. I advise caution and propose retreat — we should report this and leave it to professionals to mine the dangerous hole. Bill-E and Loch shout me down.

"We'll go slowly," Bill-E says.

"Carefully," Loch agrees.

"If there are other traps, they're probably slow burners too," Bill-E argues.

"But I doubt if there are more," Loch says. "What would be the point? One's enough. If it was set off, old Sheftree could have simply cleaned up the bodies, then set the trap again."

In the end, despite the dangers, they decide to keep going. Since they can't be swayed and there's no profit in cutting myself off from them, I reluctantly grab a shovel and all three of us climb down into the hole.

For an hour we work doggedly and fearfully — me fearful of faces appearing in the rocks, Bill-E and Loch fearful of running afoul of the dead Lord Sheftree.

We pause every time there's a rustling in the trees overhead or when a heavy stream of earth trickles down into the hole, me anticipating whispers, Bill-E and Loch thinking it might be the grinding gears of Lord Sheftree's next weapon of mass destruction. But gradually we adjust to the natural sounds of the forest and stop flinching at every minor disturbance.

Bill-E and Loch are more convinced than ever that we've unearthed the final resting place of Lord Sheftree's buried treasure. Not me. There's something magical about this hole. It drew me to it last night, sang out to the moon-affected beast I'd become, and lured it here, turning me into a conspirator, using me to clear the way for . . . what?

I don't know. I haven't the slightest idea what we might be digging our way down to. But I'm pretty certain it's not a rich miser's hidden treasure.

Loch and I work together, chipping away at the hard-packed earth around the large rocks, prying them out slowly, often painfully, rolling and dragging them up the slope.

Bill-E cleans up after us, removing the smaller rocks, pebbles, and dirt. We're an effective team, although as Loch tires from the hard work, he starts cursing and teasing Bill-E, taking out his irritation on him. At first I ignore it, but he keeps on and on, Spleenio this, fat boy that, lazy eye the other, and eventually I snap.

"Why don't you lay off him?" I snarl after an especially brutal remark about Bill-E's dead mother.

"Make me," Loch retorts.

I square up to him. "Maybe I will."

Loch holds his shovel in both hands and raises it warningly. I grab the handle and we glare at each other. Then Bill-E slips behind me and whispers, "Ice him, Grubbs!" It's so flat, so vicious, so un-Bill-E, that I turn around, startled, releasing the shovel.

"What did you say?"

Bill-E looks confused, but angry too. "I meant . . . I just . . ."

"I heard him," Loch growls. "He told you to bump me off."

"What if I did?" Bill-E bristles, and now he tries to get around me, so that *he* can go toe-to-toe with Loch.

"Stop," I say firmly. I lay my left palm against the nearest rock wall and concentrate. After a few seconds I feel or sense the vibrations of a very faint throbbing. A nonhuman throbbing. "We all need to chill."

"Who made you the leader?" Loch barks.

"We're being manipulated." His forehead creases and I start to tell him there's magic at work, affecting our tempers. But then I realize how crazy that would sound. "The soil," I say instead, inventing quickly. "There must be some sort of chemical in it. Put there by Lord Sheftree. It's making us feel and say things we shouldn't. If we don't stop, we'll be at each other's throats soon."

Loch's frown deepens, then clears. "I'll be damned," he sighs.

"The sly old buzzard," Bill-E hoots. "Chemicals to alter our dispositions and turn us against one another. Coolio!"

"I thought you were my enemy," Loch says wonderingly, staring at me. "It came so suddenly, without warning. I believed you were out to kill me. The shovel . . ." He looks down at the sharp, grey head, then drops it and clambers out of the pit. Bill-E and I follow. We find Loch sitting by the edge of the hole, shivering.

"Are you OK?" I ask.

"I don't think we should keep going," Loch whispers. "You were right. We should turn this over to someone who knows what they're doing. Chemicals . . . that's out of our league."

"No way!" Bill-E protests. "We're close, I know it. You can't back out now. That would be real craziness."

"But —" Loch begins.

"There might not be any chemicals," Bill-E interrupts. "Maybe we're just tired and edgy. It's been a long day, we're hungry, we've been working hard, it's late. . . . Combine all those things and you get three soreheaded bears."

"It was more than grumpiness," Loch says.

"Probably," Bill-E agrees. "But let's say there *are* chemicals down there. It's been so long since they were planted, their strength must have dwindled by now. I bet, if we'd dug fifty years ago, they would have blinded or killed us. Now all they can do is make our hackles rise. We should take a short break, clear our heads, then get back to work. If we find ourselves getting short-tempered again, we come up for another rest."

"I'm not sure," I mutter. If we were alone, I'd tell Bill-E about my fears — that this place is part of the world of magic. I'm sure he'd take more notice of my warnings then. But I can't speak about such things in front of Loch. "Why don't we leave it alone for today? It's getting late. Let's go home and sleep on it."

"Not yet," Bill-E pleads. "Give it until dusk, like we planned. Since we're here, we might as well make the most of the daylight."

"Spleenio's right," Loch says. Now that the influence of the hole has passed, he's his old self again, intent on getting his hands on the treasure, quickly forgetting his fears. "Let's do what we came to, then go home and relax. It might be weeks before we dig all the way to the bottom. We can't get cold feet every time we run into an obstacle."

I don't like it, but their minds are set, so after a short break, we pick up our tools and edge down into the hole again.

✠ We remove one of the biggest rocks yet and haul it to the top. Standing by the edge of the hole. Sweating, shaking, flexing our fingers. "This is torture," Loch groans.

"Think the treasure will be worth it?" I ask.

"It better be."

"What if there's nothing there, if it's just a hole?"

Loch smiles. "It isn't. We're on to something big. I can feel it in my bones."

"You're just feeling what you want to feel."

Loch scowls. "Stop being such a —"

Bill-E screams.

Loch and I bolt down the hole. We find Bill-E submerged in earth up to his waist, clinging to the rocks around him, face bright with terror. "There's nothing underneath!" he shouts. "My legs are dangling! I'm going to fall! I'm going to fall! I'm going to —"

I grab his right hand. Loch grabs his left.

"We won't drop you!" I yell.

"Not unless you give us reason to," Loch jokes.

"I was digging." Bill-E gasps, fingernails gouging my flesh. "Rooting up stones. The floor gave way. My shovel fell. I heard it clanging all the way down — a *long* way. I thought . . . I dropped this far . . . I managed to grab the edge. If I hadn't . . ." He starts to cry.

"Look at the chubster." Loch howls with delight. "Boo-hooing like a baby!"

"Can't you shut up just once in your stupid bloody life!" I roar — then catch myself. "The chemicals," I hiss. "Loch . . . Bill-E . . . take it easy. No outbursts. No insults. Relax. Think nice thoughts. Tell me when you feel normal."

"How can I be normal when I'm stuck down a —" Bill-E shrieks.

"Nice thoughts," I interrupt sternly, sensing the throbbing again, coming from the rocks around us. "Loch — you thinking nice things?"

"Yeah." Loch grins. "I'm imagining the baby's howls if we let him drop."

"Loch!"

"OK," he grumbles, and shuts his eyes. After a few seconds his expression clears. He opens his eyes and nods to show he's in control. Bill-E is less composed, but that's understandable, given the situation he's in.

"You need to talk to us," I tell him. "We're going to pull you out, but we don't want to hurt you. Are there any stones jabbing you, sticks, wire . . . anything that might cut into you if we pull you out quickly?"

"I don't think so." Bill-E sobs. "But it's hard to tell. I don't know."

"Relax," I soothe. "You're safe. We have you. Now concentrate and let us know how we can help you out of this mess with the least amount of discomfort."

Bill-E focuses and moves slightly, exploring the unseen territory around his legs. Finally he gulps and says, "I think it's safe to pull."

"Great." I smile falsely. "Loch — you ready?" He grunts. "We'll take it easy to begin with. Act on my command. Pull softly when I say. Stop if I give the order. Understand?"

"Whatever," he shrugs.

I'd like to wipe my palms dry but I don't think Bill-E would hang there patiently if I released him. So, gripping tighter, glad of the dirt on my skin that counteracts the sweat, I give Loch the nod and we tug. Resistance, but not for very long. Soon Bill-E's sliding out of the hole within the hole, trembling wildly but otherwise unharmed. When his feet are clear, we give one last yank and he sprawls on top of us, knocking us to the ground, where we lie, panting and laughing weakly.

After about a minute, without discussing it, we get up and crawl forward, eager to check out the hole that Bill-E has uncovered. It's a black chasm. Impossible to see very far down it. The light's too bad.

"Wait here," Bill-E says, scrambling up to the surface. He returns quickly, a baseball cap on his head, two small flashlights strapped to either side. "Spent half an hour last night fixing this up," he says proudly, then holds up a bigger, stronger flashlight. "I brought this too. Been lugging it around all day. Just in case."

"Spleen, you're a genius," Loch says, and Bill-E smiles. "A fat, deformed simpleton, but also a genius," he adds, and Bill-E's smile turns to a scowl.

"Why don't you take one of the lights off the hat?" I suggest. "Then we can each have one."

"No," Bill-E says. "They're not powerful enough by themselves. You need the two together for them to be worth anything." He brushes by us, justifiably smug, taking temporary leadership. He crouches by the edge of the hole he made and flicks on the strong flashlight. Loch and I crouch by him and stare. The hole continues down as far as we can see, at a slight angle, lots of little stones jutting out of the main rock face, plenty of niches for hands and feet.

"Hell," Loch gasps. "It's massive."

"There's no way Lord Sheftree could have dug this," Bill-E notes. "He might have widened the entrance to make it easier to get to this point, but the rest of it's natural."

"How far down do you think it runs?" I ask.

"Only one way to find out." Bill-E grins.

"You've got to be joking!" Loch snorts.

"What?" Bill-E frowns. "You're not coming with me?"

"We can't go down there," I mutter, taking Loch's side. "Not without good climbing boots, ropes, those metal pegs with the loops that climbers use . . . all that sort of gear."

"It doesn't look so difficult," Bill-E argues. "I say we try it and go as far as we can. If we run into difficulties, we'll come back later with climbing equipment."

"Why risk it?" I press. "Let's wait until the weekend, stock up, then —"

"You ever used any of that stuff before?" Loch asks. "Boots, ropes, and so on?"

"Well, no, but —"

"Me neither," he interrupts. "Spleenio?" Bill-E shakes his head. "If we're going to do that, we need to practice," Loch says slowly.

"So we practice. It means a delay, but —"

"What if someone comes along in the meanwhile, finds this, and claims it for their own?" Loch cuts in.

I glare at him. "I hate the way you start out on one side of an argument, then talk your way completely around to the other side."

Loch laughs. "You're too conservative, Grubbs. I share your concerns for our safety, but the Spleenster's right. If we take it easy, go cautiously, stop if we feel it would be dangerous to go on . . ."

"What if the batteries in the flashlights die while we're down there?" I ask stiffly, fighting a losing battle but determined not to give in gracefully.

"I replaced them last night," Bill-E says. "They're all fresh."

"Genius," Loch murmurs, then grins at me. "It can't be *that* deep — old Sheftree needed to be able to get up and down with his cases of treasure. The angle's not too steep. And there are loads of toe- and fingerholds."

"Let's try, Grubbs," Bill-E whispers. "We won't do anything foolish. You can call it off if you think things look dicey. We'll follow your lead. Promise."

I hesitate and check the time. Glance up to where the moon will soon be appearing. I place my right hand on the rocky floor, feeling for vibrations, but there aren't any. I think of all the dangers — then of the treasure, if it's there. If I'm wrong, if this isn't a place of magic, if I've been imagining hidden perils.

A deep breath. A snap decision. I grab the big flashlight from Bill-E. "Let's go."

THE CAVE

✠   ✠   ✠

DESCENDING slowly, testing each foothold firmly before setting my weight on it. Coming down three abreast, me in the middle, Loch on the left, Bill-E on the right. Loch complains several times about not having a light of his own, but Bill-E refuses to relinquish either of his. I've been to his house. I know that Ma and Pa Spleen keep several flashlights around the place, ever fearful of power outages, determined never to be left stranded in the dark. He could have easily brought another one for Loch. A mistake or intentional oversight? I don't ask.

It's stuffy down here, warmer than I imagined. The air's not so bad though. I thought it would be stale and thin, but there's a good supply of it. Easy to breathe.

Part of me knows this is crazy. It screams from the back of my head, reminding me of what happened last night, the face, the whispers, the throbbing today. It wants me to assert myself, demand we make for the surface, tell Dervish, leave all this for experienced spelunkers to explore.

But a larger part thinks it's thrilling. We're the first humans to come down here in decades. In fact, if the others are wrong, and this wasn't used by Lord Sheftree, maybe we're the first people to *ever* find it. Maybe it will turn out to be an amazing geographical feature and we'll get to name it and be on the news. Reni would really dig being a celebrity's girlfriend.

You're an idiot, the cautious part of me huffs with disgust.

"Put a sock in it," I grunt back.

✠ I lose track of time pretty quickly. Have we been down here ten minutes? Twenty? The hands of my watch are luminous, so I could check. But I'm not going to start fiddling around in the dark, rolling up my sleeves, leaning forward to squint. I'm keeping both hands on the rock face and all my senses focused on the climb.

I go carefully, one hold at a time. Foot-hand-foot-hand-foot-hand-foot. Bill-E and Loch are the same. We don't speak. My flashlight hangs from my right wrist by a strap. The light bounces off the rocks. I'd have to stop, turn around, lean back, and point the light down to get a clear view of what lies beneath. But I'm not going to do that. I'm taking no chances. The thought of slipping . . . sliding . . . tumbling into the unknown . . .

Foot-hand-foot-hand-foot-hand-foot-ha —

I touch ground. Or a very large overhanging rock. Can't tell yet. "Wait," I call softly to the others, who are slightly higher than me. "Let me feel around a bit. I think . . ." I extend my foot outwards. More rock. I tap it — solid. Gently lower my other foot, still holding tight to the wall. Gradually letting my full weight shift to my feet, I release my grip and stand unsupported. The ground holds and my stomach settles.

Bringing up my flashlight, I shine it around and gasp.

A cave. Not the largest I've ever been in, but a reasonable size. Lots of stalactites and stalagmites. A waterfall to my right. I should have heard the noise before now, except my breath and heartbeat were heavy, muffling my hearing.

"Grubbs," Loch hisses. "Are you OK? What is it?"

"I'm fine," I whisper, then raise my voice. "It's a cave." I shine the light on the floor around my feet, making sure I've truly struck bottom. I spot the shovel that Bill-E dropped. "It's OK," I tell my friends. "You can come down."

They detach themselves from the wall and stand beside me. The light from Bill-E's hat mingles and crosses with mine, and we gaze around in awed wonder.

The formations are beautiful, some of the most incredible I've ever seen. Water drips slowly from the tips of many stalactites, so this is an active cave, still growing. I recall lectures from a couple of class trips to caves. It can take thousands of years for spikes to form. Thousands more for them to alter. If I lived to be a hundred and came back here just before my death, this cave would probably look no different than it does right now.

"It's amazing." I sigh, taking a step forward, head tilted back, looking up to where the roof stretches high above us. "How can this have been here all this time . . . hidden away . . . nobody knowing?"

"The world's full of places like this," Bill-E answers even though I wasn't really asking him. "We only see a fraction of what's there. People find new caves, mountains, rivers, all the time."

"OK," Loch says loudly, shattering the mood. "It's a lovely cave, beautiful, glorious, la-dee-da-dee-dum. But I don't see any treasure."

"Moron!" Bill-E snarls. "*This* is the treasure. You couldn't buy a cave like this, not with all the gold and diamonds in the world."

"I don't want to," Loch says sourly. "What good's a damp, dirty cave? I'll settle for the gold and jewels." He looks around and spits. "If there *are* any."

Bill-E turns, temper fraying. I speak up quickly. "He's right, Bill-E. Not about the cave not being worth anything — it's amazing, beyond any price. But we came looking for a different sort of treasure. We should check to see if it's here. If it isn't, that doesn't matter — we'll still have found the cave. But if there's treasure too, all the better."

Bill-E relaxes. "Yeah, let's look. The cave isn't that big. If there's treasure, it shouldn't be too hard to find."

We move forward, three explorers in wonderland. Even Loch looks impressed, although he isn't blown away by the cave's beauty in the same way as Bill-E and me. We touch the rising pillars, fingers coming away damp. In certain places the stalactites and stalagmites have grown together to form giant, solid structures that join the floor and ceiling. One is wider than the three of us put together, a monster resembling a couple of massive chimneys.

"I've never been down a cave without a guide, or in such a small group," Bill-E says after a while. "It's strange. Quiet. Peaceful."

"Hey," Loch grins. "You know my favorite part when I'm in a cave? It's when they turn the lights out, so you can see what it looks like pitch-black."

"No way!" I say quickly.

"Uh-uh!" Bill-E chimes in.

"What's the matter, ladies?" Loch laughs. "Scared of the dark?"

Bill-E and I share a look. Neither of us wants to switch the flashlights off. But Loch's smirking goadingly. If we don't meet his challenge, we'll never hear the end of it.

"Go on," I mutter to Bill-E. "You first."

He gulps and turns one light out, then the other.

The cave feels much smaller now, more threatening. It's probably my imagination but I believe I can sense shapes in the shadows, waiting to form fully in the darkness, so they can leap forward and pounce on us unseen. My finger hovers over the switch on my flashlight. I'm torn between not wanting to look like a coward and not wanting to fall prey to forces of magical malevolence.

Before I can make a decision, Loch does it for me. "What a sissy," he crows, then reaches over, jams my finger down hard, and jerks it backwards, quenching the light.

My heart races. My breath stops. The walls seem to grind shut around me. In a panic I try to turn the flashlight on, but my finger's numb from where Loch pressed down on it. I can't find the switch! I can't turn the light on! The shapes are coming! In a second or two they'll be upon us, all claws, sharp teeth, and . . .

Bill-E switches one of his flashlights on. He's chuckling weakly. "That was cool."

I look around — nothing. The cave looks exactly the same as it did before. I was imagining the danger. I force a short laugh and switch my light on, then press ahead with Bill-E and Loch. We continue exploring.

✠ After half an hour I don't feel too hot. It's nothing to do with the temperature of the cave — it's warmer down here than it was on the surface — but with the time. I check my watch to confirm what I already know — it's night. High above, hidden from sight by the layers of rock and earth, the moon's rising, and tonight it's as full as it's ever going to be.

I get the same sick feeling as last night and the night before, only stronger, relentless. In horror movies, people sometimes don't change into werewolves unless they see the moon — if it's hidden by clouds or they're locked away it doesn't affect them. But that's crap. The moon's a powerful mistress. She can reach through any wall or covering and work her wicked charms.

Bill-E and Loch are bickering about the treasure and whether or not it's here. Loch doesn't think it is — we've been around the cave a few times and found nothing — but Bill-E still insists it could be.

"You don't think Lord Sheftree would have left it lying on the floor for anyone to stumble across and walk off with, do you?" he argues. "He'd have thought about somebody finding the cave, either by digging down like we have, or maybe through some other entrance he didn't know about. He'd have hidden the treasure, stuck it out of sight, so that even if strangers wandered in by accident, they wouldn't find it, not unless they actively searched for it."

"So where do you think it is, geni*ass?*" Loch sneers. "We've looked everywhere. Unless it's invisible treasure, I don't think —"

"We've looked nowhere," Bill-E shouts, and his voice echoes tinnily back at us. "Some of the larger stalagmites might be hollow," he says, quieter this time. "The treasure might be buried in one of them."

"There's an awful lot of stalagmites," Loch says dubiously.

"We have time," Bill-E smiles. "And maybe it's not down here at all." He points up at the walls. "There are ledges, holes, and tunnels, maybe smaller caves — or, for all we know, *bigger* caves. This could be nothing more than the entrance to a system of huge, interlinked caverns. We still have lots of exploring to do. We've only scratched the surface."

"Let's do it another time," I mutter, head pounding, feeling as though I'm surrounded by a layer of fire. "It's night. Time to go home."

"Not yet," Loch snaps. "I don't have to be home for a few more hours."

"Bill-E . . ." I groan.

"Well, Gran and Grandad will be expecting me back soon," he says. "But it's not like I've never been late before. I'll tell them I was with you, that we lost track of time — which isn't a total lie."

I want to scream at them. The fools! Can't they feel it? Even through my sickness, with a brain that's being hammered to a pulp by a searing headache, I can sense danger. The throbbing's back, stronger than ever. We need to get out now, quick, before . . .

Or am I imagining the danger, like I imagined the monsters

in the dark? Maybe it's just my sickness that we have to fear, and this is only a beautiful, eerie cave.

Even so, if I turn into a werewolf here, that's more than enough for any pair of humans to worry about. Trapped underground with a supernaturally strong wolfen beast, Bill-E and Loch wouldn't last five minutes.

"Look," I snap, "we have to go. We'll come back tomorrow and explore some more. But it's dark up top — it's night. We said we'd go when the moon rose." I stop, gather my thoughts, and try a different approach. "We don't want to draw attention to ourselves. If we come home late, caked in mud and dirt, what will everyone think? If they start asking questions . . ."

"He's got a point," Bill-E concedes. "Gran and Grandad put Sherlock Holmes and Watson to shame. We should play it safe, act normally, especially if we're going to be coming here a lot."

"OK," Loch sighs. "But one more search before we leave." He points to the top of the waterfall, where it comes gushing out of the sheer rock wall fifty feet above the cave floor. "Up there, those large holes. We can climb up pretty easily. I want to have a peek at them. Then we can go."

"I dunno," Bill-E says. "They're fairly high, and that wall's steeper than the one we climbed down."

"What's a wall to three hardy explorers like us?" Loch laughs. "It won't take long. And if the treasure's there, we can go home on a total, triumphant high."

"Grubbs?" Bill-E asks.

I shake my head violently. I think I'm going to throw up. I'm trembling helplessly. Climbing's the last thing on my mind.

"Are you all right?" Bill-E asks, training his twin lights on me.

"Some kind of bug," I gasp. "I've had it for the past few days."

"Maybe we should get him home," Bill-E says.

"Sure," Loch grunts. "Right after we've explored above the waterfall." He slaps Bill-E hard on the back. "Come on, Spleenario — last one up's an asswipe!"

The ploy works. Bill-E forgets about me. They race to the wall and climb. Loch's laughing, teasing Bill-E, roughly urging him on. I turn my back on the pair, leaving my flashlight pointing in their direction, to provide some extra light for them. I stumble away and sink to my knees. Lean my head against one of the smaller stalagmites and groan softly. I feel like a corpse that's been stuck in a microwave to defrost, half frozen, half on fire. I try to control my breathing, to think calm thoughts, but my head's full of wild, animalistic images — running, chasing, ripping, fangs, blood.

I stare at my fingers — they're curling inward. I can't straighten them, no matter how hard I try. I search within for magical warmth, the energy I've drawn upon over the past forty-eight hours, but it doesn't seem to be there for me now. Maybe the cave's got something to do with that. Or maybe I'm just out of fighting spirit. Out of resistance. Plumb out of luck.

"Not . . . going . . . to . . . turn," I snarl. Thinking of Loch and Bill-E, what I could do to them. Cursing myself for being so weak, not going to Dervish when I had the chance, allowing this to happen. I see now that it was fear, plain and simple. It didn't matter what state Dervish was in, I should have told him the minute he got back. I kept the news to myself because I was scared of what he'd do. I was hoping the charms of the moon would pass, that I was just ill, imagining the inner struggle. The same fear that kept me from learning the ways of magic stopped me from telling my secret to Dervish. Grubbs Grady, coward of the century. And now Bill-E and Loch are going to pay the price for my cowardice.

I try yelling a warning, telling them to stay up high, where I can't reach them. But my throat won't work. The vocal cords are constricting, thickening, cutting off my air supply. I guess, since wolves can't talk, they don't need all the throat muscles that humans do.

I pull my head back from the stalagmite, meaning to run, get to the surface if I can, before I change. Put space between myself and my friends. *Lots* of space.

But then I see the face again. It's in front of me. Bulging out of the stalagmite, as though carved out of rock. A girl's face. Similar to Gret's, as I noticed before, but not hers. Different. Younger. Darker hair. Smaller. Eyes and lips closed. Like a death mask.

The whispering, stronger than last night, more insistent. Certain words break through, but they're not words I know. A foreign language. Harsh and fast.

I'm staring at the face, listening to the whispers, held firm to the spot, feeling myself change, when suddenly —

A scream. Behind me. At the waterfall.

As I turn towards it, there's another scream. Then a very loud thud.

Then nothing.

I race across the cave, grabbing the flashlight on the

way, lycanthropic fears momentarily forgotten, blocking out thoughts of the face and sounds of the whispers. There's a body on the ground and it's not moving. That's where all my concerns are now.

I reach the body and gently turn it over. It's Loch. Face ashen. Eyelids flickering. Mouth opening and closing softly.

"Loch?" I murmur, holding his head up, trying to see how bad the damage is. I feel something wet and sticky smeared around the back of his head. I don't have to check to know that it's blood.

Scrabbling sounds. Bill-E hits the ground hard, feet first, having jumped from a spot a few yards above. "Is he OK?" he shouts, panting hard.

"I don't know. What happened?"

Bill-E gulps, kneels, stares at Loch's head and my bloody hands. "He fell," Bill-E croaks. I almost can't hear him — the whispering's louder than ever, the words coming fast and furious. "We were climbing. He slipped. I . . . I reached for him. He wasn't far away. I grabbed. But he fell. I couldn't catch him. I tried but I couldn't . . ."

"It's just as well that you didn't," I comfort him. "He'd have dragged you down with him. Take off your coat." Bill-E gapes at me. "For under his head."

Bill-E shrugs off his jacket and balls it up. While I hold Loch's head, he lays it underneath, then I softly lower Loch down. His eyes haven't opened. He's breathing raggedly. This isn't good.

"I told him not to go up there," Bill-E says hollowly. He's crying. "I warned him. But he wouldn't listen. He thought he knew it all."

"Hush." I'm calmer than my brother. I've seen worse things than this. Blood doesn't alarm me. "One of us has to go for help. The other needs to stay here, sit with Loch, look after him."

"I'll go," Bill-E says quickly. "Please, Grubbs, I don't want to stay. Not in this cave. It's too dark. Please don't make me —"

"OK," I shush him. "You can go. Find Dervish. Tell him what happened. He'll know what to do. But run, Bill-E. Run!"

Bill-E nods, stumbles to his feet, stares at Loch's face, opens his mouth to say something, then races for the exit. I hear him scrambling upwards, but only barely, over the sound of the whispers, then turn my attention on Loch and the dark pool spreading out from beneath his head and Bill-E's blood-soaked jacket.

✤ Talking to Loch. I'm babbling — about school, the treasure, vacations, girls, wrestling. I've put my coat and sweater over him. Have to keep him warm.

His breathing comes jaggedly. His eyelids have stopped twitching. His heartbeat's irregular. I keep on talking, rubbing his arms and chest, but I don't know if I'm doing much good.

The sickness is still in me. My head feels ripe to burst. Sometimes my words come out as growls, and my fingers clench while I'm rubbing Loch, digging into his cold, clammy flesh.

I fight it. Search within for warmth, energy, magic —

anything. I can't change, not until Dervish comes, not until Loch's in an ambulance, on his way to the hospital, safe.

"Won't turn," I snarl, slapping my cheeks one after the other. "I'm not a wolf. I can control myself. Won't let the moon . . ."

Loch shudders. His breath stops. I thump his chest hard, then remember first aid classes at school. Opening his mouth, I press firmly down on his chest, then release him and count. One, two, three, four. Press and count again. A third time. I place my lips over Loch's. Breathe out, so that his cheeks puff up. Withdraw. Press — two, three, four. Press — two, three, four. Press — two, three, four. Mouth-to-mouth.

Trying to remember if I'm doing it right. Was it three presses on the chest, or four, or five? Should I blow air firmly down Loch's throat or —

Loch coughs and breathes again.

I sink back, whining with relief and fear. That was too close. This can't be happening. We were looking for treasure. Messing around. Loch was teasing Bill-E. Everything was normal. You can't suddenly go from that to a life-or-death situation like this.

Except I know from past experience that you most certainly *can.*

Besides, things weren't normal — the face, the whispers, the throbbing, the sense that we were in danger. I should have been more forceful. Made them leave. Insisted they go home.

The sickness within me grows.

The noise of the whispers increases.

Loch's blood continues to flow.

✠ Still talking. Telling Loch he's got to stay alive for Reni's sake. "She'll be a mess for years if you die," I sob. "Trust me, I know what losing a sister does to your head. You can't leave her, Loch. She needs you."

It feels like hours since Bill-E left. Loch stopped breathing again a few minutes ago. I resuscitated him, but it took longer than the first time. I was in floods of tears by the end of it, sure I'd lost him.

What's keeping them? Damn it, they should be here by now. Don't they know how perilous this is, how much danger Loch's in? I can't keep him alive forever, not by myself. If they don't —

Loch's breath stops again. Cursing, I start with the chest pressing and mouth-to-mouth. The beast within me wants to suck in air, not breathe it out. It wants to draw the life from Loch, feed on all that blood around his head and shoulders, sip from that terrible pool, dark in the dim light of the flashlight. If I drop my guard, just for a few seconds, there's no telling what it — *I* — would do.

The whispers increase. It's like I'm being shouted at now. I want to roar back at them, but I need all my breath for Loch.

Press — two, three, four. Press — two, three, four. Mouth-to-mouth.

Nothing's happening. I don't panic. It was like this last time. I just have to keep going, stay calm, stick with it. He'll revive eventually.

Press — two, three, four. Press — two, three, four. Press . . .

It doesn't work. No matter how much I press and breathe, Loch doesn't respond. His face has shut down. His lungs don't move. His heart is still.

Third time unlucky.

"No," I whisper. "I don't accept this. He can't be . . . *No!*"

I bring my hands up, meaning to press again, harder than before, wildly. But something about Loch's expression stops me. It's peaceful, calmer than it ever was in life. Staring at him, I know with total, awful certainty — he's lost. I could press and breathe from here till doomsday and it wouldn't make the slightest bit of difference.

Loch Gossel is dead.

✠ Stumbling around the cave. The whispers deafening. Tears streaming down my cheeks. The wolf within me howling to be set free. Loch dead. Muttering, "This can't be happening. This can't be happening. This . . ."

My right foot hits either a large stone or small stalagmite. I fall flat. As I'm picking myself up, the face of the girl forms in the floor in front of me. Her expression is the same as Loch's. I gaze at her in horror. This is what Loch will be like for all eternity, or at least until his body rots. Blank, lifeless, ever still, ever serene, ever —

The girl's eyes snap open. Her lips part. She shouts at me, words I can't understand.

I scream and propel myself backwards. Scream again. Halfway through, it turns into a howl. With an effort, I force the howl down, then fix my eyes on the face in the floor.

"No," I snarl, pressing my hands hard against the sides of my head. *"NO!"* I roar.

Something shoots out of me. A force I haven't felt in all its power since I fought Lord Loss and his familiars in *Slawter*. I shut my eyes, feeling energy zap out of me. The scream rises and rises. I feel as if I'm floating above the ground. I think that if I opened my eyes I'd find that I *am* floating. I hold the scream, the cords in my throat feeling like they're going to burst, until . . .

A sound like cannon fire. Then sudden silence. The scream dies away. My head flops. I collapse. My hands come away from my head, to protect my face from the fall.

When I sit up, I'm breathing hard and crying. But the whispering has stopped. I glance at the spot in the floor. The girl's face has disappeared. And I don't feel sick anymore — only small, lonely, and scared.

Standing, I shine the flashlight around, trying to pin down the source of the cannon fire. It only takes a few seconds to find it — a large crack in one of the walls, close to the waterfall, that wasn't there before. Did I divide the rock with my magical scream, or is the crack coincidence, the result of air flowing into the cave or a change of temperature? I don't know. At this particular moment, I don't really care.

I stagger over to Loch and slump beside his lifeless form. Impossible to believe he'll never move again, or laugh, or wrestle. You think your friends are never going to die, that all the people you know and care for will be with you forever. Then the world makes an idiot of you, so quickly, so simply, that you wonder whether any of your family or friends will survive another day intact.

I want to bring him back. I want to shake him, kick him, pump magic into him, make him breathe, make him live. It should be easy, like starting a stalled car or a crashed PC. There should be rules, instructions, things you can do. But there aren't. When it comes to humans, death's death, that's that, and you're a fool if you think any different.

Crying, I lean over Loch to hug his empty shell and tell him how unfair this is, how good a friend he was, how he shouldn't be dead, how much I want him to live, how scared I am. And it's only when I grab his shoulders and haul him up, pulling his head in towards my chest, that I realize — his head, the coat, and the area around his shoulders . . . they're all dry.

At first, I'm so distraught I don't understand why that should be so strange, why it strikes me as being out of place. I'm about to dismiss it, to banish it from my thoughts, when the significance hits and I do a confused, incredulous double take. Then, because I still can't make sense of it, I cry the question out loud, in case giving it voice will help me find an answer.

"Where the hell has all the blood gone?"

PART TWO

✠   ✠   ✠

JUNI

THE PROMISE

✠ ✠ ✠

DERVISH regards the cave with something close to religious awe when he enters. For a long minute he doesn't even glance at where I'm hunched over Loch. His attention is fixed on the walls, the roof, the formations, the waterfall. Then Bill-E nudges him softly and mumbles, "Over there."

Dervish snaps to his senses and advances. "Billy told me what happened," he says, still several yards away. "How is he?"

"Fine —" I say, and Dervish smiles "— for a dead man." The smile vanishes. He slows. Behind him, Bill-E covers his mouth with his hands, stifling a sob or a scream.

"You're sure?" Dervish asks softly.

"Check for yourself," I say hollowly. "Prove me wrong." My face crinkles. *"Please."*

Dervish kneels and gently pushes me away. He examines Loch. Rolls his eyelids up. Puts his ear to the dead wrestler's chest. Goes through all the same resuscitation tricks that I tried. I don't bother telling him that he's wasting his time. Let him find out for himself.

Eventually he draws back, saddened — but worried too. He looks at me. Then at Bill-E. "Tell me again what happened."

"He slipped," Bill-E moans. "I tried to grab him but I couldn't reach."

"There was nobody else in the cave?" Dervish presses sharply. He looks at me and licks his lips. "*Nothing* else?"

"No," Bill-E cries.

"No," I whisper.

"You're sure?" Dervish asks, voice low, directing the question just to me this time. "It's important. You were alone? The three of you? You're *sure?*"

I nod slowly, confused.

"I tried to save him." Bill-E sobs. "But he was too big. Even if I'd caught him, he'd have dragged me down with him, right, Grubbs? It wasn't my fault. Please, Dervish, don't say it was my fault."

"Of course it wasn't," Dervish sighs. "It was an accident." He rubs his chin, troubled. He stands, looks around, glances at the waterfall and the spot Loch fell from. Doesn't mention the crack — he hadn't seen the wall before I howled and split the rock, so he assumes it's a natural feature.

"Is there anything you can do?" I ask. "Any spells . . . ?"

"No," Dervish says plainly. "He's beyond help."

I fight back tears. "Will the ambulance be here soon? Maybe they —"

"Nobody can do anything!" Dervish snaps. "He's dead. You've seen death before. Don't ask the impossible. You're not a child."

I stare at my uncle, stunned by his harsh tone. It sounds

like he's criticizing me for caring about my friend, as though that's wrong.

Dervish catches my look and his expression softens. "This is bad. And not just because Loch is dead." He looks around again, nervously. "I didn't call for an ambulance."

"What?" I explode. "But —"

"He's dead," Dervish says as if that explains everything. "An ambulance wouldn't have helped."

"But you didn't know that when you came," I shout. "When Bill-E came to get you, Loch was alive. Why didn't you call for help? Maybe they would have gotten here before you. Maybe Loch would be alive if —"

"Billy, come here," Dervish interrupts me. Bill-E approaches slowly, fearfully, trying not to look at Loch. Dervish keeps me silent with a fierce frown. I want to scream bloody murder but I bite my tongue, waiting to hear my uncle out. When Bill-E's a few feet away from us — the closest he's going to come — Dervish speaks.

"What happened tonight is a tragedy. I feel for you, honestly, even though I'm not showing it. We'll talk about this afterwards. I'll give you all the support I can, make it as easy for you as possible. But right now I have to be hard. And I have to ask something hard of you."

He pauses. Again a nervous glance around. "As far as the official verdict goes, Loch can't have died here," Dervish says. "I'll explain later. Right now you have to trust me. We need to move the body. Make it look like this happened somewhere else. Cover up the entrance to the cave and tell nobody about it. Understand?"

Bill-E and I gape at him.

"Please," Dervish says. "I wouldn't ask if it wasn't crucial."

"You want to . . . tamper . . . with the body?" Bill-E croaks.

"I just want to move it," Dervish says. "We'll take it to the quarry. You can say you were climbing there. We'll call the emergency services once we —"

"What the hell, Dervish!" I yell. "Loch is dead, and you're playing games? What sort of heartless —"

"You're not listening!" Dervish roars, losing his temper. He glares at me. "Let me say it again — this is *crucial*. This cave has been hidden for hundreds of years for a very good reason. It must be hidden again."

"Hidden?" I whisper, and Dervish nods. "You mean you knew about it?"

"I didn't know the exact location, but I knew it existed." Dervish is white-lipped. "The entrance was deliberately blocked off many centuries ago. We'll have to fill it in again." He stands and offers his left hand to me, his right to Bill-E. I don't want to take it but his eyes tell me I must. Bill-E is even slower to accept the hand, but eventually he takes it too.

"You have to promise," Dervish says. "Promise you'll back me up, lie for me, say this happened in the quarry, tell nobody about the cave. On all that's holy to you . . . in the name of your dead mothers . . . promise."

"And if we don't?" I ask stiffly.

Dervish smiles bitterly. "I could force you, but I won't." He squeezes our hands tightly. "You both know that we live in a world that's not the exclusive domain of humans. There are other forces. Demonic forces. This cave could be valuable to them. If we don't handle this right, demons will benefit, and Loch won't be the only one who dies. *Will you promise?*"

Neither of us says anything.

Dervish sighs wearily. "I'll tell you more about it later. You can retract your promise then if you feel I didn't have good reason to ask for it. But there isn't time now. We have to work quickly, get Loch to the quarry, and call the police immediately. If we delay, it will show up on the autopsy. It'll be risky, no matter how we play it, but if we don't act now, while we have the advantage of time, it will be a lot harder. For all of us."

Bill-E and I share a look. Neither of us knows what this is about but we trust Dervish. He's saved both our lives in the past.

"You swear you'll explain?" I ask, voice shaking hoarsely.

"I swear."

"Then I promise."

Dervish smiles gratefully and looks to Bill-E.

"OK," Bill-E says weakly.

"In the name of your mother?" Dervish presses, hearing a wavering tone in Bill-E's promise.

Bill-E hesitates, then nods. "In the name of my mother."

Dervish relaxes and lets go of our hands. "Thank you. This is more important than either of you can possibly realize. It's . . ." He looks down at Loch and gulps, then mutters under his breath, "At least there wasn't any blood."

That reminds me about the mysterious disappearance of Loch's blood. I start to tell Dervish about it . . . then stop. It isn't important. The blood must have simply seeped through cracks in the ground. I'll only confuse the situation if I speak up now.

Dervish bends beside the body, gently touches Loch's pale forehead, then sighs and tugs at his beard. A moment's pause, during which I see how hard he's having to work to cover up his true feelings. Then his expression firms and he moves into professional mode. "Billy, you bring the flashlights. I'll take the shoulders. Grubbs, grab his legs. And for hell's sake, don't drop him — that's the last thing we need."

✠ The next few hours are nightmarish. We carry the body home, load it onto the back of Dervish's motorbike, strap the arms around Dervish, and put a helmet on it so if anybody sees Loch it'll look like he's a living passenger. Shivering next to Bill-E, I watch them drive away, then go inside and try to drink a mug of hot chocolate in the kitchen. But I'm unable to gulp it down.

Dervish comes back for us. Usually he'd only let one of us ride behind him, but there's no time to follow the rules of the road. At the quarry, Dervish throws Loch over the highest edge of the cliff. The dull thump as he collides with the hard floor brings tears to Bill-E and me. I don't know why Dervish didn't chuck Loch down when he brought him out here. Maybe he wasn't thinking straight. Or maybe he wanted our tears, to make the rest of the charade seem more realistic.

I make a phone call. Following Dervish's instructions, I dial the emergency number, report the accident breathlessly, give my details, and wait. I wonder why Bill-E and I didn't do that before. We both have cell phones. Why didn't one of us climb out of the cave and call for an ambulance? Did we simply lose our heads and panic? Or did something in the cave control our actions?

The police arrive before the ambulance. Dervish debated whether he should stay with us or go home and return after the emergency services got here. In the end he chose to stay, instructing us to tell them that we called him after calling for help. Everybody here knows Dervish. They know how fast he goes on his bike. The police are always trying to catch him, but he's too crafty. They'll assume he tore over here at top speed. They won't like it, but given the tragic circumstances they're hardly going to make a fuss.

Paramedics examine Loch. They do what they can to bring him back to life. But they go about their job sluggishly, without hope, knowing it's too late. They don't cover his face before loading him into the back of the ambulance, because they don't want to upset Bill-E and me. But as soon as he's out of our sight, I'm sure the sheet will be pulled up and over.

The officer in charge asks to take our statements. Dervish clears his throat and gently suggests calling Loch's parents first. The officer blushes — he's young, probably hasn't seen a corpse before, temporarily forgot his training. Dervish offers to make the phone call. The officer accepts the offer with a grateful smile.

Dervish keeps it quick and to the point. There's been an accident. Loch's been taken to the hospital. Says it's serious. Doesn't say Loch's dead. Leaves that for the doctors. Not the sort of news you should break over the phone.

Home. The police drive Bill-E and me. Dervish follows on his bike. More hot chocolate. I still can't drink it. Biscuits that I can't eat. Dervish turns on the heat. While the police are talking with us, Dervish calls Ma and Pa Spleen. They arrive before we're finished, splashing out on a taxi for maybe the first time in their lives. Anxious to protect their grandson. Eager to whip him away from the police and their questions. Dervish has to drag them aside and explain that it will be easier if they let the police finish — if we don't do it here, we'll have to go to the police station later. He takes them into the kitchen and plies them with tea and coffee. I imagine them discussing me, Ma and Pa Spleen blaming me for Bill-E being in the quarry after dark, saying I'm responsible for him risking his life on such a dangerous climb — and for Loch's death.

The interrogation goes softly. The police don't suspect foul play. They just want to get the facts straight. We tell them we went for a walk. Wound up at the quarry. Went climbing. Loch fell. Bill-E tried to catch him. Couldn't. The end.

Kids fool around at the quarry all the time. Every few years some local official vows to block it off. Nobody's ever followed up on the promise, though I think they will after this. The police take the attitude that a fatality was bound to happen sooner or later. Just bad luck that it happened to us.

They leave not long after midnight. (How did it get so late, so quickly?) They say they might return to take follow-up statements, but that shouldn't be necessary. They tell us to take a few days off school, maybe go away for a while. They warn of a possible backlash — parents sometimes overreact in situations like this. Loch's relatives might blame Bill-E and me, hurl insults and accusations at us. The police say we shouldn't be too upset if that happens, to try to understand their position.

Bill-E wants to stay the night, hear Dervish out, learn why we had to lie. But Ma and Pa Spleen are having none of it. They want out and fast. They've never liked Dervish and aren't much fonder of me. Bill-E's arguments are shot down before they're out of his mouth. Then it's into the back of the taxi that they've kept waiting, and home, where they can pour poison in his ear and remind him of all the times they warned him about the grisly Gradys, how we'd led him astray.

Then it's just me and my uncle, alone in our old mansion. A foul smell in the air — the stench of lies and deception.

Without discussing it, we retire upstairs to Dervish's study, where we sit on opposite sides of his huge desk, facing each other, me suspicious and wiping away tears, Dervish ashamed and tweaking the hairs of his beard.

Time for explanations.

COMING CLEAN

✠   ✠   ✠

YOU know about the Demonata," Dervish begins. "You've seen them at work. You know of their powers, their magic, how destructive they are. You know that some, like Lord Loss, can cross between their universe and ours."

"Does this have anything to do with *him*?" I croak.

"No. He doesn't need the cave, and from what I know of him, he isn't interested in it." Dervish stops for a moment, thinking about the best way to proceed. "Lord Loss is an exception. Most demons can't cross easily between universes. If they could, this world would be awash with the Demonata, and humans would be their playthings and slaves.

"Many demons hunger for that. They spend a large portion of their time trying to open windows between the two universes. They find weak points where crossing is easier and work on them, assisted by power-crazed mages on this side. The Disciples try to stop them. We look for focal points, prevent crossings where we can, deal with the aftermath when we can't."

"Like in *Slawter*," I nod. "You explained all that to me before. But what about the cave?"

Dervish puffs his cheeks up, then blows out air. "More than a millennium and a half ago, the Demonata invaded. Normally they cross singly or in small groups. The demons hate one another almost as much as they hate humans — infighting is rife. But in this case thousands banded together to launch an all-out assault. They set out to create a large, permanent opening — a tunnel instead of a temporary window. The cave was the focus of their attempt.

"They were helped by a twisted druid. Our world was more magical then. Magic is an energy, and like any form of energy it can ebb and flow over the course of time. Back then it flowed strongly through this world. There were many more magicians and mages than there are now, though they called themselves druids and priestesses. It's a source of debate as to why there's so little magic in the world these days. I guess —"

"You're rambling."

Dervish grins sheepishly. "Sorry. Keeping it simple, the Demonata tried to open a tunnel through the cave. They nearly succeeded. From what we know, many did cross over, but only lesser demons. The tunnel was shattered before the masters could cross, and the cave entrance was later filled in and hidden from the world, so nobody could make an attempt there again.

"Since that time a watch has been kept on this area. There's always been a watcher here — even before the Disciples were formed — monitoring the situation, making sure the cave isn't reopened. I'm the latest in a long line of watchmen. That's why I don't wander the world like most Disciples. I get away to deal with other matters occasionally, but the cave is my main priority."

"But you said you didn't know where it was. How could you keep people away from it if you didn't know its location?"

"Powerful spells were cast when the cave was filled in. As watcher, I would have known instantly if anyone tried to gain access. The spells would have led me straight to the cave."

"Then why didn't you come as soon as we started digging?" I frown.

Dervish's left eye tics. "The spells didn't work."

"But you said —"

"Something went wrong," he snaps. "That's why I was so worried. I thought a powerful mage must be at work, one with the ability to override the protective spells. When you told me Loch was dead, worry turned to outright panic. Before the tunnel can be reopened, a sacrifice must be made. If Loch had been murdered, the magical potential of the cave would have been reactivated, allowing the Demonata to start building a new tunnel."

"That's why you wanted to know if there was anybody else in the cave," I note.

Dervish nods and licks his lips. "I'm still concerned. Those spells were cast by a magician — they *should* have worked. You didn't see Loch slip, did you?"

"No."

"So you can't be certain there wasn't somebody else present, that he wasn't deliberately killed."

"Bill-E was with him. He would have seen if there'd been anyone else up there."

"Maybe," Dervish says dubiously. "But if there *was* somebody, and they were powerful enough to mute the warning spells when the cave was reopened, they might have been invisible, or used magic to wipe their presence from Billy's memory."

I smile weakly. "You're seeing phantoms where there aren't any. We only broke through to the cave today — yesterday, I mean. We went down by ourselves as soon as we discovered the entrance. There couldn't have been anybody else."

"You're right," Dervish sighs. "I'm jumping at shadows. But I'm so wired! Back when the tunnel was open, only lesser demons were able to cross. But the core of the tunnel was widening all the time. It had almost gotten to the point where the masters could cross. The shell of that core remains intact. If the Demonata ever restored it, thousands could cross in a matter of days, masters and all."

"Couldn't you force them back again, close it like before?" I ask.

Dervish makes a face. "Humans are much less magical now than they were the last time it was open. And back then they only had to deal with weaker demons. We could stop it happening if we caught wind of it in advance, but if they opened it without our knowing . . ."

He trails off into silence. It's hotter than normal in here. Dervish doesn't usually have the heat on this late. The temperature reminds me of the time we fought Lord Loss in the cellar, the unnatural heat of the Demonata's universe. I feel highly uncomfortable and shift around nervously in my seat.

"What happens now?" I ask quietly.

"The cave will need to be hidden again. Fresh spells will

have to be cast, and we'll try to find out why those in place before didn't work. But that's a job for a magician. I'll put out the call and we'll wait."

"I thought there weren't magicians anymore, only mages."

Dervish shakes his head. "There's one. He's the head of the Disciples, though we don't have much to do with him personally — he fights most of his battles in the Demonata's universe. I fought alongside him once, a long time ago. He gave me the task of guarding this area a few years later. I don't know how long it will take him to come, but hopefully it won't be more than a month or two."

"Are we safe while we wait?" I ask nervously. "What if an evil mage finds the cave and makes a sacrifice?"

"It's not that simple," Dervish says. "The tunnel can't be opened instantly. A sacrifice would have to be made to start the process, then over the next few weeks the entrances would fuse with the core. At that point someone would need to conduct a lengthy, complicated ritual in the cave. I'd feel *that* magic at work — it would be impossible to hide — and I'd move heaven and hell to stop it. But I don't think we have anything to fear. Since I wasn't warned by the spells when you broke through to the cave, nobody else would have been. The Demonata don't know the entrance to the cave has been cleared, so they have no reason to move on it."

"Then we're safe?" I watch his face closely in case he tries to lie.

"As safe as we've ever been," Dervish says calmly, and there's no hint of deception in his features. I start to relax slightly. He raises a finger. "But regardless of how safe it is, I don't want you going back to the cave."

"As if!" I lick my lips. "What happens when you block it off again?"

Dervish shrugs. "Life will go on as normal. I'll stay here, keeping watch, and another Disciple will replace me when I'm old and grey and of no use anymore."

"What about Bill-E? Are you going to tell him what you told me?"

"Yes. As soon as Ma and Pa Spleen let him out of the house — which might not be anytime soon." Dervish stands and stretches. "What a night. I'll be glad to see dawn."

"Loch won't ever see dawn again," I mumble. It's not fair that I'm having to think about the cave, demons, and magic when I should be thinking only about my poor dead friend.

Dervish smiles helplessly and comes around the desk. Lays a comforting hand on my shoulder. "You can talk with me about him if you want. I know what it's like to lose a friend. I can help."

"Yeah. Maybe. Thanks." I take a deep breath and look up. The fear grows in my chest. It tries to grab my tongue and hold it still. It whispers caution. Screams for silence. But I have to tell him. I can't keep it secret any longer.

"There's more than Loch and the cave that we need to discuss."

"Oh?" A puzzled little smile, not expecting anything major.

"I think I have the family curse." His smile freezes. I push the fear down deep and spit out the words I never wanted to say. "I think I'm turning into a werewolf."

✠ I tell Dervish everything — the sickness, the party, the bottle, the magic that's been growing within me since

Slawter. Waking to find myself at the entrance of the cave, digging as if my life depended on it. The whispers, the face in the rock, splitting the wall with my scream.

Dervish listens silently for the most part, eyes dark, chewing his nails or stroking his beard. Occasionally he'll ask me to elaborate, to describe the sickness and whispers in more detail. But most of the time he just watches me, his expression impossible to read, head cocked slightly, like a priest hearing confession.

A long pause when I finish. Then Dervish tuts like a teacher. "You should have called me back on Saturday or told me as soon as I got home."

"I know what I *should* have done," I snap. "But I didn't. I was afraid you'd make me become a Disciple if you knew about the magic. And I hoped I was wrong about turning into a werewolf. Keeping quiet was dumb, but I never claimed to be an Einstein. So cut me some slack." I glare at him but he only stares back calmly. *"Well?"* I grunt when he doesn't say anything. "Am I turning or not?"

"I don't know. The signs you describe suggest it, but . . ."

"What?" I hiss.

"Victims don't realize," he says quietly. "Nobody turns into a werewolf overnight. It's a gradual process, spread out over three or four months. The kids often know things aren't right — if they wake covered in blood, or lying naked outdoors — but I've never heard of anyone being conscious of the change or actively fighting it. When they start to turn, their minds blank out. They can't remember changing or do anything to stop it. What you describe is unlike anything any other member of the family has ever reported. And we've been dealing with this for a *long* time."

"You're saying maybe it isn't . . . ?" I feel hope blossom in my chest.

"I don't know," Dervish says again. "The signs all point to lycanthropy — the distorted face, the hands clenching, the howling. If somebody else had seen it happening to you, I'd say you were definitely damned. But you shouldn't be able to note these things yourself. It . . ."

He gets quiet again. His forehead's a landscape of worry lines. I've thrown him big-time. He looks even more perturbed than he did in the cave. At least he knew where he stood with that, and what he had to deal with.

"Tell me about the magic again," Dervish says. "Everything you can recall."

I go through the weirdness one chunk at a time. Waking to find myself levitating above the bed. Reversing the flow of water down the sink. Moving things with my mind. Making the bottle rise, explode, and transform into flowers and butterflies.

"Everybody saw that?" Dervish asks. "Billy will confirm it?"

"Of course." I frown. "Why?"

Dervish grunts. "If we're lucky, you're losing your mind, imagining the magic and the change. You've had a hard few years, been through a lot — more than just about any kid in the world. Maybe it's caught up with you. Maybe you're going . . ." He twirls a finger around in the air at the side of his head.

"Know what I like most about you, Uncle?" I ask waspishly. "Your subtle tact."

"Stuff that! This is no time to be soft. If you're going crazy, I'd be delighted, because we could deal with it, get help, fix what's wrong. Nobody's seen most of this magic you say you've been working. It could all be in your head. But if you really did those tricks with the bottle and there are witnesses . . ."

"There are," I say stiffly. "And there's the cave. We found it on Sunday. We only dug down a little bit, but when we returned yesterday it had been excavated. Rocks and dirt everywhere. Bill-E will confirm that too. *I* did it, Dervish. I went there, not entirely human, and burrowed down."

"Any idea why?" Dervish asks.

"No. Unless it was the whispers . . . the face . . ."

Dervish makes a long humming sound. "If you're not crazy — and much as I hate to admit it, I don't think you are — I've no idea what the face means. Unless some spell was cast upon the cave long ago, one I don't know about." He scratches his left ear, then the right. "You couldn't recognize anything the girl was saying?"

"No."

"Did the whispers seem to be drawing you to the cave or warning you off?"

I think about it. "Warning me off. But if that was the case, why was I there? What made me go back and dig? Could it have been the Demonata? Calling to the beast I'm becoming? Using me to open a tunnel between universes, so they could cross?"

"Possibly," Dervish says. "I wouldn't have thought they had that kind of power, but if it's true that you're turning, and if there's magic involved . . ." He frowns and trails off into a very troubled silence. I let him brood for five minutes . . . ten . . . twelve. Then I can't stand it any longer.

"What are we going to *do?*" I cry. "I don't want to turn into a werewolf. I don't want to hurt anyone. But —"

"Quiet," he shushes me. "Let's not jump to conclusions. There's a lot going on that's strange to us. But I can ask around, get advice, search for answers. You haven't turned and you haven't hurt anybody, so don't work yourself up. That won't help."

He takes a sheet of paper off a pile on the desk, balls it up, and tosses it from one hand to the other, thinking. "First, I mount a watch over you every night. If you feel the sickness returning — or anything that doesn't feel right — you tell me instantly. If you feel magic forming, tell me that too." He hesitates. "Can you do anything now? A small spell?"

I shake my head, scared of even trying.

"If I could see you in action . . . pinpoint the source you tap into . . . it might help establish what we're dealing with."

I shudder, then nod and focus. I stare at the ball of paper that Dervish is still throwing from hand to hand. I try using magic to knock it off course, so it falls to the floor. But nothing happens.

"I can't do it," I say after a minute. "It isn't there now. It comes and goes."

"OK," Dervish smiles. "Don't knock yourself out. Now, it's been a long, tiring night. Let's get you to bed and I'll keep an eye on you."

"But the change . . . the magic . . . that's it? We're just going to leave it?"

"Sure," Dervish says, then smiles reassuringly. "We're not

going to figure this out tonight. There's not much I can do until I see evidence of your transformation or magical prowess. When that happens, I should have a clearer idea of what you're going through, and we can take it from there. Right now the best thing you can do is hit the sack and get some sleep. The problems will still be there tomorrow, but we'll be in a better state of mind to deal with them."

Since that's all there really is to do, I take Dervish's advice, get ready for bed, then slip beneath the covers. Dervish sits in a chair by the circular window, keeping watch, protecting me, just as he did when I first moved into this house. Maybe it's his calming presence, or maybe it's simple exhaustion, but within minutes, despite everything, my eyes droop and I slip into unconsciousness.

Just before I go under completely, I remember the one thing I didn't tell Dervish about — the blood disappearing from beneath Loch's head. I don't think it's important but he should be told, just in case I'm wrong. I try to rise but it's too late, I'm too far gone.

Dreams.

�֍ I jolt awake. My eyes snap open and I lurch upright in bed. But it's not like waking from a nightmare. No racing heart or afterimages of a bad dream. It's more like somebody jabbed me with a blunt knife and stung me out of sleep.

I stare around, confused, not sure why I woke so quickly. Then I see that Dervish is gone. That's probably what disturbed me — he slipped out for a few minutes to get something, go to the bathroom, change clothes, or whatever, and I sensed him leave. It alarmed me and I jerked awake. Simple.

I start to lean back, half smiling, then stop. There's more to it than that. Something's wrong. I have the feeling of being in danger.

I get out of bed warily and pad to the doorway. There's a light in the corridor at the top of the staircase. I slip out of my room and head for the light. The house is warm — Dervish hasn't turned the heat off.

I think of calling Dervish's name but don't. If we're not alone, if we're under attack, I don't want to tip off our enemies. I don't think the situation is that grave — the feeling of danger isn't overwhelming — but it pays to be cautious.

I reach the wide, ornate staircase that links the three floors of the mansion. Darkness below. A dim light above, coming from the direction of Dervish's study. I home in on it.

Moments later I'm standing outside the study door, which is ajar. Dervish normally shuts the door, but tonight he left it open, probably because of the heat. He's talking on the phone. If the door had been shut, I couldn't have heard what he was saying. Open like this, I can hear him perfectly.

"Yeah," he grunts softly, "I know." A pause. "I don't think so. I didn't explore it fully, but . . ." Another pause. "That's why I said I don't *think* so. I'll go back tomorrow, check it thoroughly, and . . . Yes. No. No. They said there was definitely no one else there." A pause. "Of course I can't be certain. I wasn't there. But I trust them. We're safe. I'm as sure as I can be, without being one hundred percent."

Dervish fidgets on his chair. I think he's maybe heard a sound and is coming to check. I start to back away but then he speaks again.

"Just let him know what happened." A pause. "Yes, I know

the consequences if . . . Yes!" Snappish now. "I'm not a fool and I'm not new to this. In my opinion we're safe. But only one person can confirm that. And he will, when he comes. But he can only do that once you get off the phone with me and pass on the message." A pause. "I know he's not easy to get in touch with. I know I'll have to wait. But the sooner you start, the . . ."

Silence. A long pause this time. I hear Dervish tapping the desk with his fingers. Finally, softly, he says, "He's like my son." I stiffen and move forward a few inches. "Of course, if the worst comes to . . . Yes, I know. I *know*. But I'm hoping . . ." Dervish sighs. Another long silence.

If I lean forward I can see him. There's a black folder on the desk close to his hand.

"I have the numbers," he says quietly. He stops tapping and draws the black folder closer to him. Doesn't open it. "Yes, I can do it. I have the strength. If there's no other . . . if it comes to it."

Another silence, which Dervish breaks curtly with, "Just tell him. You do your job, let me worry about mine."

He slams the phone down and gets up.

I race back to my room. Dive under the covers. Pull them up over my chest. Try to look like I'm sleeping.

Dervish returns. Checks that I'm OK. Sits in the chair again. I lie very still, eyes closed, listening intently. Finally, after several long minutes, there's the sound of light snoring.

I sneak out of bed. Tiptoe past the dozing Dervish. Head back upstairs in the dark, not turning any lights on. I think I know what is in that black folder and why I woke with the sense of danger. But I want to make sure. I couldn't see clearly. There's a slim chance it's something else.

The study. The door's still open. I slip inside, gently shut the door, find the desk in the dark, and turn on one of the smaller lamps. The desktop lights up. The folder's still there, close to the phone, black as the cave was.

I pick it up and cradle it in my hands, staring at the blank cover, knowing what I'll find when I open it, praying to whatever gods there are that I'm wrong.

Then, with a snap, I flick the cover back. I find several pages, a handful of names, addresses, phone numbers, and e-mail addresses on each. And at the top of the first page, not in large letters, bold print, or underlined, but standing out anyway, as if they'd been burned into the paper and were still aflame, the two words that confirm all that I feared.

The Lambs.

MISERY MARK II

✠   ✠   ✠

I spend the rest of the week off from school. Strangely enough, I'd rather go. It's boring as hell hanging out at the house all the time, brooding, only Dervish for company. I want something to take my mind off Loch's death and all the other stuff. I want to be with my friends, talk about the tragedy, put it behind me, get on with life. But it's expected that I take the week off to recover, so I do.

✠ I try hard not to think about the folder or the Lambs. Like Dervish said, the curse has been in our family a *long* time. Some parents kill their own children if they turn, but many can't bring themselves to be executioners. Generations ago, the Lambs were formed to deal with that problem. The wealthier members of our clan founded and continue to fund them. It's their job to kill teenagers who've turned into werewolves. They also experiment on some of the beasts, in the hope of unlocking the genetic secrets of the family curse and curing it.

Dervish doesn't have much to do with the Lambs. He doesn't trust them. He always planned to kill Bill-E or me himself if the worst came to pass — there's nothing like the personal touch. But my uncle's been through a lot these past few years. He looks as strong as ever, but looks can be deceiving. Maybe he doesn't feel he has the strength to deal with me if I turn.

I don't like the Lambs either. I've only met one of them, but she was a cold, creepy woman, and the whole idea of letting strangers put me down like a wild dog fills me with distaste. Dervish has made it clear in the past that he would put me out of my misery if such a drastic step was ever called for. I can understand why he might want to retract that promise now, but understanding doesn't make it any easier to accept. As childish as it might seem, I feel like he's betrayed me.

✠ Bill-E manages to come over on Thursday, after Dervish argued hard on the phone for a couple of days to persuade Ma and Pa Spleen to let him out of the house. He looks shell-shocked. Pale and sickly. His lazy left eyelid flutters so much, it looks like worms are wriggling beneath the flesh. He doesn't say much, which is unusual for Bill-E. Listens numbly while Dervish explains about the cave and why we had to move the body. Doesn't seem too bothered by the threat of a demon invasion.

"I called Loch's house," Bill-E says when we're alone in the TV room. I stare at him, not sure how to respond. I wanted to phone Reni all week but didn't dare. "His father answered," Bill-E continues. "I could tell he'd been crying.

I wanted to say sorry, ask how they were, if there was anything I could do. But I couldn't speak. My mouth dried up. In the end he put the phone down. He didn't get angry. He just sounded sad."

Bill-E's staring off into space. The way this has hit him, you'd think it was his best friend who'd died, not a bully he didn't like. But maybe that's why it's harder for him than me. Guilt's mixed up with grief. I think he's sorry for all the bad thoughts he had about Loch, the foul names he no doubt called him behind his back, the times he probably wished his tormentor was dead.

"I'm going back to school on Monday," I tell Bill-E. "What about you?"

He shakes his head. "I don't know."

"You should. It might help."

"Gran and Grandad don't want me to. They said I can stay at home as long as I want. Said they'd hire a private tutor."

The meddlesome, selfish old buzzards! I probably shouldn't be too hard on them. They're old and lonely. Bill-E's all they have. I can understand why they want him to themselves, locked up safe where they can fuss over him twenty-four/seven. But they should know better. He needs to be out in the real world, getting back to normal as soon as possible.

"I remember you telling me about when your mom died," I say softly. Bill-E looks at me, eyes coming into focus. "Your gran and grandad kept you indoors for a year. You didn't speak to anybody else. You fought with other kids who tried to talk to you."

"Then I got whacked in the jaw by a boy in a store," Bill-E laughs jerkily.

"And that set you straight." I sit beside him. I think for a moment of putting an arm around him but decide against it — no need to go overboard. "Don't cut yourself off from your friends, Bill-E."

"Do I have any?" he asks sadly.

"You know you do," I snap. "Maybe not as many as you wish, but there are plenty of people who like you and feel sorry for you, who'll help you through this. But they can't if you shut yourself off, if you let your grandparents smother you. Come back to school. Move on. You know it makes sense."

"Loch can't move on." Bill-E sighs.

"No," I agree stiffly. "He can't. But *we* didn't die in that cave. We're alive. Loch isn't, and that's a wretched shame. But life goes on. Loch goes to a grave, we go back to school. That's how it has to be."

Bill-E nods slowly. "Are you going to the funeral?"

"I don't want to, but I think I need to."

"I can't," Bill-E whispers. "I can go back to school, but not . . ."

"That's OK," I smile. "School will be torture enough."

Bill-E returns the smile briefly, then stares off into space. "I can still hear his scream," he mutters. "And I can see his face. His eyes . . . He didn't know he was going to die. There wasn't terror in his expression, just worry. And a bit of anger. He should have looked more terrified. If he'd known . . ."

We sit there for hours after that, TV off, sniffling occasionally, but otherwise as silent as Loch must be.

✠ ✠ ✠

✠ Friday. The funeral. It's horrible. And that's all I'm saying about it.

✠ Monday. School. Everyone staring and whispering. Kids scurry out of my way. It's like the Grim Reaper's walking next to me.

I spot the gang in one of our usual hangouts behind the cafeteria, taking shelter from the rain. Talk dries up as I approach. When I stop, they stare at me, I stare at them, and for a few long seconds nothing is said. Then Charlie breaks the silence with, "Loch must have been mad as hell, looking down on his funeral — he hated flowers. And having to wear a suit too!"

Everybody laughs.

"You're an ass, Charlie," Frank giggles.

"Don't say anything like that in front of Reni," Shannon warns him.

"Please," he huffs. "I'm not a *total* jerk."

The laughter fades. Frank clears his throat. "Was it really bad?"

"Crapville," I say tightly.

"Did he say anything before he . . . you know?" Mary asks.

I nod soberly. "His last words . . . I had to strain to hear them . . . he . . . ." I cough and everyone leans in close to listen. "He said . . . his voice a painful croak . . . fighting for breath . . . eyes locked on mine . . . 'Mary Hayes has a face like a cow's dirty rear.'"

Mary roars with fury and clubs me with her bag. The others laugh. Then the bell rings and we march into class. Back to normal — or as much as it can be.

✠ A rumor at lunchtime. Misery Mauch has gone on sick leave. A mental breakdown. Some say he was overcome with grief when he heard about Loch, but that's rubbish — Loch never went to see Misery. Apparently he's been replaced by a woman. They say she's quite young, though nobody's had a good look at her yet — she's been in Misery's office most of the day.

I don't see Bill-E during lunch. He's with the new counselor. I hope she has more of a clue than old Misery. Bill-E needs professional help, not some overeager do-gooder. I'll have to check her out, make sure she's not going to mess him up even further. Grubbs Grady — rooter-out of frauds!

✠ Halfway through geography, a freshman kid delivers a note to my teacher. The new counselor wants to see me. Guess I'll get to give her the once-over sooner than I thought.

I'm kept waiting outside the office for a few minutes before I'm called in. The counselor is standing by the side of Misery's desk when I enter, her back to me. When she turns round, I almost drop through the floor.

A slender woman of medium height, in her late thirties or early forties. Well dressed, more like a businesswoman than a teacher. Pretty but not gorgeous. Very little makeup. Pure white hair tied back in a ponytail. Extremely pale skin. Pinkish eyes. She's an albino. But that's not what knocks the wind out of my sails. It's the fact that I know her and last saw her

a year ago in Slawter frying the brains of a demon collaborator named Chuda Sool.

"Juni Swan!" I cry.

"That's Miss Swan to you, young man," she says with a little smile. Then steps forward and wraps her arms around
me, hugging me tight while I stand frozen, stunned, staring
down at the top of her pale white orb of a head.

✠ Juni was one of film producer Davida Haym's assistants. A
psychologist, it was her job to make sure the children on-set
were being well treated. Dervish fell for her, and I think she
had a thing for him too. I doubt the pair got beyond lovesick
looks and holding hands, but I bet they would have if life
hadn't gone crazy on us all.

When hell hit the fan and the demons ran wild, Juni helped
us break a hole through the barrier that Lord Loss had
erected around the town. Without that gap, everyone would
have perished. She was knocked out during the fighting and
only recovered when the barrier had closed again, trapping
hundreds of members of the cast and crew inside. Like the
rest of us, she was helpless and had to stand by, watching
and listening as the demons tortured and killed them.

She lost herself to fury and found that like me she could
tap into the magical energy in the air. In a fit of rage she used
this power to kill Chuda Sool, a demon collaborator who'd
slipped through the gap. She regretted it afterwards. Snuck
away in the night, leaving a note for Dervish saying she was
confused and filled with sorrow. Said she might contact him
someday if she straightened her head out, but not to expect
to hear from her again.

Now here she is, filling in for Misery Mauch, looking a bit more strained than when I last saw her, but otherwise no different.

"Why are you here?" I gasp once I've recovered from my initial shock. *"How?"*

"That's what Billy asked." She chuckles. We're sitting in front of the desk, chairs close together. Juni's holding my hands. "Aren't you pleased to see me?"

"Of course. But it's been so long. I never thought . . . And how did you wind up here, in our school? You're not a guidance counselor. Are you?"

"Not exactly." She sighs and lets go of my hands. "It's not a long story or particularly complicated. My head was in a mess after our experiences on the film set." She pauses. Her eyes make flickering contact with mine and I get the message — don't mention the demons or the slaughter. *Please.* "It took me months to recover," she continues, "but not as long as I thought. I realized early on that work would help, that I needed to be busy, that by helping others with their problems, I could help myself too.

"A friend offered me a job involving school work. I became an adviser to a network of counselors. I supervised them, provided them with guidelines, helped out with their problems, organized meetings and conferences. The school network I initially covered was far from here. Then, a couple of months ago, I was given an opportunity to relocate. I knew your school would be part of my new network. To be honest, that's largely what drew me to it."

She smiles weakly. "I've been wanting to get in touch with Dervish since the day I ran off. I haven't because of fear, guilt, shame. This was a way to take a step closer. I meant to ease myself into his life, observe from a distance for a while, work up the courage to face him again. Then William Mauch got sick just when you and Billy most needed a compassionate and understanding ear. As his superior I was expected to step in for him. As your friend I felt compelled to. So . . ." She shrugs, embarrassed. "Tah-dah!"

"Dervish will be happy," I grin. "He missed you."

Her face creases. "Please don't tell him. Not yet. Not until I'm ready."

"But —"

"Please." She stops me, sharp this time. "I'll see him soon but not right now. Not until I've had time to settle in, get my bearings, and finish what I came here to do."

"What do you mean?"

She leans forward, eyes warm but serious, and says, "I want to talk about your friend, Loch Gossel." Puts a small, thin hand on one of my large, knobbly ones. "I want to discuss his death and how that hurt you."

✠ We talk for almost an hour about my friendship with Loch, what he was like, how he died, what I felt, how I've coped since then. I feel awkward at first, but Juni listens patiently, asks all the right questions, never pushy, always sensitive. She doesn't pretend we're not old friends, but at the same time she treats me like a patient, the way a professional should. No falseness, no charade, not smarmy. I find myself opening up to her, telling her things I haven't even told Dervish, about my pain, my nightmares, my loss.

We talk about Bill-E a lot. She spent most of the morning

with him and she's worried. "I can't tell you everything that we talked about," she says. "I have to respect his privacy. But I got the feeling there was animosity between him and Loch. Would you say that was an accurate assumption?"

"They didn't get along," I admit.

"Did they ever fight?"

I smile. "No."

"Why the smile?"

"Loch was almost as big as me. A wrestler. It wouldn't have been much of a fight."

"But they argued?" she presses.

"Loch . . ." I hesitate, not wanting to say anything bad about my dead friend.

"He teased?" Juni guesses.

"Yeah. He picked on Bill-E. Sometimes he was cruel. I didn't like that but I couldn't do anything about it. It was Bill-E's problem, not mine."

"Was Loch teasing Billy on the day of his death?" Juni asks. She's not afraid to talk about death openly. Doesn't hide behind softer terms like "incident" or "accident." I like that.

I think about it. "A little bit, yeah. But we were tired from di — I mean, from climbing in the quarry. We were all a little cranky."

"They didn't fight?"

"No."

"You didn't argue with Loch or try to stop him from teasing Billy?"

"Not really."

"You're sure?"

I shrug. "I don't remember everything that was said. The

hour or two before he fell is kind of blank. I'm not blocking it out. I just . . . it's like, when I look back, I'm looking through a mist. Do you know what I mean?"

Juni nods. "I know exactly what you mean. Part of my job will be to help you pierce that mist."

"Does it matter that much?" I frown.

"Absolutely. It could be a mist of guilt. If you said something ugly to Loch that you regret now, you might have buried it. If you don't deal with that, it could lie within you for years, then work its way back to the surface, hurting you, making you feel horrible about yourself."

"Is that what you're doing with Bill-E?" I ask. "Piercing the mist?"

"Yes. Although it will be harder with him than you. You're not the still-waters-run-deep type."

"Huh?"

"You're honest and straight. What one sees is what one gets. Loch's death hurt, but I don't think it struck you to the core like Billy. You're made of tougher stuff, Grubbs Grady. Tougher than Billy and tougher than me. I doubt we'll have any serious problems. You're too plain to be complex."

"You might be wrong," I mutter, annoyed at being described that way. "Maybe I just do a good job of covering up my pain and confusion."

"Perhaps," Juni says. "But don't worry, I make no rash assumptions. If you *are* suffering deep inside, I'll find out and help. You have my word on that."

We talk a while longer about Loch's teasing and what I thought of it. Then a bit more about the day he died, how long I held him, my efforts to keep him alive, my feelings when I realized he was dead. I cry at that point. Juni makes no move to comfort me, just sits, watching, waiting. When I recover, she hands me a tissue to wipe my cheeks dry, then moves on.

At the end of the session she stands and shakes my hand. When I try to pull away, she grips tight, pink eyes finding mine and holding them. "Billy promised not to tell Dervish about me. If you can't make that promise or feel strange about it, please say so. I want to be the one to tell him I'm here. I'd rather do it later, when I'm ready, but if you feel like I'm putting you in an awkward position, I'll do it now."

"No." I smile. "I'll keep it quiet. He doesn't take much of an interest in school life. If he asks, I'll tell him some nutty dame replaced Misery Mauch. I bet he won't even ask for your name."

"Thank you." She releases me. "We'll talk again tomorrow if you don't mind."

"I'd like that."

She smiles broadly, then ushers me out, leaving me to wander back to class, head buzzing, lips lifting at the edges, feeling for the first time since Loch's death that there might be a touch of silver to what previously seemed to be a bleak, black beast of a future.

HOME VISIT

✠   ✠   ✠

Bɪʟʟ-E improves over the next few days. He starts talking again, loses that faraway look in his eyes, stops moping around like a zombie. He sings Juni's praises whenever we meet. Tells me how closely she listens, how she understands him perfectly and says the right things at exactly the right moments.

"I never saw her in action in Slawter," he says as we trudge out of school, Thursday afternoon. "I didn't realize how cool she was. I thought it would be weeks, maybe months, before I could smile again. But look at me!" He grins widely. "She's a miracle worker."

I smile, slightly strained, ridiculously jealous. I've seen Juni every day but our sessions have been brief. She's spending far more time with Bill-E than me, and when we meet, she talks more about Bill-E's feelings than my own.

"I feel like I can say anything to her," Bill-E gushes. "She's like . . ." He stops. We're about to turn a corner. There's a bum sitting on the pavement, his back against the wall, head low, face hidden by a bushy beard and straggly hair. Bill-E reaches into his right pocket, then his left. Finds some change and holds out his hand. The tramp doesn't respond immediately, then reaches out without looking up. Bill-E drops the coins into the bum's hand and smiles. The guy doesn't smile back. Bill-E shrugs and moves on.

"Where was I?" he asks.

"Discussing the miracle worker," I grunt.

"Oh, yes!" And he's off again, Juni this, Miss Swan that. I want to snap at him to shut up, he's driving me crazy with his fan talk. But that would be cruel and childish of me. And I'd only be saying it because I envy the hours and secrets they share.

✠ Friday. I try getting Juni to take more of an interest in me. I tell her about my parents and Gret, what my emotions were when they were murdered and how I felt after all the killing in Slawter. I run her through a few of my grislier nightmares. I expect her to jump at this fresh information and pump me for all the juicy details. But I expect wrong.

"That's ancient history," she says. "I don't think it's relevant now."

"But I thought it was all linked," I sputter. "The past . . . the present . . . that what I felt then influences what I feel now."

"Of course," she says. "But I believe you've dealt with the past adequately. Your nightmares are natural, a healthy way of releasing tension and confronting your fears. I see no reason to reopen old wounds. Don't you agree?" She waits, one eyebrow raised.

I shift awkwardly in my seat, blushing.

"It's not a contest, Grubbs," Juni says quietly. I stare at her uncertainly. "My time isn't something you need to fight with Billy for. My relationship with Billy in school is the same as with you — purely professional. I spend more time with him because he needs me more. There are others who need me too. I've met with several students over the past week, including Loch's sister, Reni, at her home."

"You've met Reni?" I ask, startled.

Juni nods. "Like I told you on Monday, I'm not an ordinary guidance counselor. My work takes me outside the classroom. Reni is really suffering. But she's coping. She'll be back in school next week. And when she comes, I'll be spending time with her here. Which means I'll have even less time for you. That can't be an issue."

"Of course it isn't. I never . . . I didn't . . ."

"It's all right," she smiles. "Jealousy is normal, even in a boy your age."

"I'm not jealous," I huff.

"Maybe not. But if you are, it's OK. We can't help irrational feelings. The important thing is to recognize such feelings and not allow them to fester. I don't want a rift to develop between you and Billy."

"I don't know what you're —"

"Grubbs," she interrupts, "I'm being blunt because I respect you. This is how I'd address an adult. If you want, I can treat you like a child and tiptoe around these issues. But if —"

"OK," I cut in, angry but cool. "It's no big deal. I understand. I can keep a handle on my . . ." I scowl, then spit it out. "My jealousy."

"I'm glad to hear it." Juni smiles, patting my right hand. "Now that we have that out of the way, let's talk some more about Billy and what you, as his best friend, can do to help him manage his pain."

✠ Marching home, thinking about what Juni said. She saw through me as if I was made of glass and knew exactly how to deal with me. She's in a different league from Misery Mauch. Every school should have a counselor like Juni Swan, someone who can really connect with —

A man steps out in front of me and I almost crash into him. I have to take a quick step back. It's a homeless person. He's standing in the middle of the narrow path that leads from Carcery Vale to my home. He's staring at me with small, dark eyes. Very hairy. Smells bad. Dressed in shabby clothes that are thirty or forty years out of date. Wears a small bunch of flowers in one of his upper buttonholes. They look ridiculously out of place.

"Excuse me," I mutter, trying to inch my way around him. He doesn't react. I take a more cautious look — we're alone, nobody in sight, flanked by trees. My warning senses kick in. I prepare to run or fight if I need to. But the man makes no threatening moves. Just stares at me, saying nothing, hands by his sides, eyes steady.

"Could you . . . ?" I make a sign for him to move over. But he still doesn't budge. Sighing, I step off to the side, trampling down a patch of weeds. I wave sarcastically at the clear path. The bum nods at me slowly, then walks past.

Shaking my head, I get on the path again and head for home. I've taken no more than five or six steps when I remember the bum from yesterday, the one Bill-E gave money to. I turn to give him the once-over, wondering if it's the same guy. But the path is empty. No sign of him. He must have slipped back into the forest. It's like he disappeared.

✠ Homework. Struggling with a complicated chemistry formula when somebody knocks at the front door. I gratefully close my textbook and go see who's there, happy for an excuse to take a break.

It's Juni.

"Hello, Grubbs," she says nervously. "Is your uncle in?"

"Yeah. But . . . um . . . I thought you didn't want to see him yet."

"I didn't." She laughs lightly. "Then, on my way to my hotel, I found myself taking a left instead of a right and I ended up here." She shrugs. "I guess the part of me that makes the big decisions thinks that it's time."

"Do you want me to call him, or would you rather go find him yourself?"

"Call him, please. It would be more polite."

"Dervish!" I bellow, then gesture for Juni to enter. "May I take your coat?" I ask as she steps inside.

"Thank you." She takes it off and passes it to me. Her fingers tremble as we touch. I think about taking hold of her hand and giving it a friendly squeeze, but before I can, Dervish comes trotting down the stairs from his study.

"There's no need to roar," Dervish grumbles. "I'm not deaf. I can . . ."

He sees Juni. Comes to a complete halt, left foot in midair. His jaw slowly, comically drops.

"Hello, Dervish," Juni says, waving awkwardly. "I'm back."
And they blink at each other like a pair of startled owls.

✠ Two hours later. Dervish and Juni have spent the time shut inside the TV room. I've been in the kitchen, where I'm still stuck on the same chemistry problem. Not that I've been trying hard. Most of my thoughts have been devoted to Dervish and Juni, and the things they might be discussing.

Part of me wants to creep to the door and eavesdrop but that would be sneaky and unfair. I'd hate it if somebody did that to me, so I'm not going to do it to them.

✠ About half an hour after that, when Juni's gone to the bathroom, Dervish pops into the kitchen. He puts the kettle on, prepares two mugs, grabs some cookies, then sits beside me. He's grinning softly. "You should have told me," he says, but there's no anger in his voice.

"She asked me not to," I reply.

"I know, but . . ." He chuckles. "No. It doesn't matter. Maybe it was better this way. The shock was nice. I'm just glad I didn't fall down the stairs and break my neck." He looks at me. "Juni told me about the counseling — without revealing any of the confidential details. Said you're doing great, all things considered. She thinks you're a marvel. Said if everyone had your powers of recovery, she'd be out of a job."

I shrug like it's no big thing, but the compliment tickles me.

"Billy's not so lucky." He sighs. "I knew Loch's death hit him hard, but I didn't realize things were this bad. I thought, after *Slawter*, he'd be prepared for death. He seemed to handle that OK. But Juni says he bottled up his feelings, that his reaction now reflects a delayed reaction to what happened then."

"She's the expert, I guess."

Dervish nods slowly, then says, "Billy told her I was his father."

"Oh?" Bill-E doesn't know that his mother had an affair with my father, that I'm his half brother, that Dervish is his uncle. He thinks Dervish is his dad.

"She normally wouldn't share information like that," Dervish goes on, "but this was one time she felt she had to. She needed to know if it was true."

"What did you tell her?"

"The truth. Well, some of it. I didn't mention Cal or your relationship to Billy. That's our secret. I didn't see the need to reveal that much."

The kettle boils. Dervish pours water into the two mugs. Glances at me as he's dunking tea bags. "I thought you might have told Billy about your Dad."

"No," I say softly.

"You know that you can if you want? It's your call, not mine."

"I know. I want to tell him and I will. But I've never found the right time. It's the sort of news that will turn his world upside down. I've been waiting for a quiet, uneventful period, but we haven't had any over the past few years."

Dervish picks up the mugs and pauses. "I wouldn't wait too long. You know better than most people that time is precious. Waiting's a dangerous game. Sometimes you miss the boat and end up regretting it."

I nod thoughtfully. "I'll give it a few months, let Bill-E get over Loch. When I think he's ready, I'll sit him down and spit it all out."

"If you want any help . . ."

"I'll ask. Thanks."

We smile at each other. Then Dervish heads back to the TV room to continue playing catch-up with Juni.

✠ Eleven. Juni's still here. At her invitation I've joined her and Dervish in the TV room. They're sitting together on the couch, not touching but *very* close. They're chatting away as if they hadn't seen each other for decades. They hardly ever toss a question or comment my way. I feel like a third wheel but I don't mind. It's fun watching them. I've never seen Dervish so gushy. Didn't think the bald old coot had any romance in him.

They talk about all sorts of things — school, Carcery Vale, motorcycles, bands, films, TV. For a man who's never shown any interest in music, movies, or sitcoms, Dervish has become awfully knowledgeable all of a sudden.

"You were at that gig too?" Juni squeals — yes, *squeals!* — when talk turns to a punk band they both liked. "I don't believe it. What a small world. I was in the pit — what about you?"

"Backstage," Dervish says modestly. "I knew one of the roadies. He got me a pass. Actually, I used to hang out with the lead singer when we were younger."

Dervish hanging out with punk front men? Moshing backstage at concerts? It's official — I've stepped through into a parallel universe.

"I'm going to bed," I mutter, rising and faking a yawn. I normally don't hit the sack before midnight, but this is getting too surreal.

"Bed?" Juni blinks and checks her watch. "Goodness. How did it get to be so late? I have to go. I need to get up early in the morning."

She stands. Dervish is on his feet a split second later. "Not yet," he gasps. "It's only eleven. That's not late."

"It is for me," she laughs.

"But I haven't shown you around the house yet." He throws it out in desperation, as if she must see the house now or self-combust. "You said you wanted to see the upstairs, didn't you?"

"Yes," Juni says hesitantly, looking at her watch again. "Perhaps another time?"

"It won't take long," Dervish smiles. "A quick tour. You can come back for a better look later."

"Perhaps you won't invite me back again," Juni murmurs, lowering her lashes demurely. Yipes! What a line! You can't get much cornier than that.

"You can visit anytime you like," Dervish simpers. I stand corrected on the corniness front.

"Well . . . OK," Juni decides. "But it *will* have to be quick — fifteen or twenty minutes tops. Agreed?"

"You can have it in writing if you want," Dervish smirks.

"No," Juni says and touches his hand. "I trust you."

Talk about love-struck puppies! This is excruciating. Any more sappiness and I might vomit.

✠　✠　✠

✠ I accompany Dervish and Juni around the mansion, hanging back a few feet, grimacing like an old crone every time one of them makes some lovey-dovey coo or comment.

Dervish is superanimated, whisking her through the maze of corridors and rooms, treating her to brief sound bites about the house's history. She loves the cellar — she's a big wine connoisseur too.

"You'll have to come uncork a few bottles with me," Dervish insists.

"Wine is made for sharing," Juni agrees.

"I was just about to say that," Dervish says excitedly. "I can't believe how much we have in common."

"I know," Juni smiles. "The same bands, movies, books, wine . . . It's freaky."

She sounds a lot younger when she says things like that. I've noticed that in adults before. People learn a new way of speaking as they grow up, but words and phrases from their childhood pop out sometimes, taking them back twenty or thirty years in the space of a couple of syllables.

Upstairs the tour continues, although now they're talking more about bands and books, less about the house. I think of injecting some cutting remark — "Maybe you're really twins who were separated at birth" — but why spoil their fun? Besides, the more I let them babble, the more ammo I'll have to tease Dervish with later.

We come to Dervish's study. The lights and PC are still on from when he was in there earlier. The door's ajar. Juni's slightly ahead of Dervish and starts to go in ahead of him. Dervish doesn't mind. He's smiling serenely. But then he remembers the spells. (I think of them before he does but wickedly choose not to say anything, thinking how much fun it will be if she turns into an elk or a zebra.)

"Juni, no!" he barks. She stops short, surprised. He smiles shakily. "I mean, it's a mess in there. Please let me go in first and . . ."

He tries to press past her but she puts up a hand and stops him. "Wait." She frowns at the door, then takes another step towards it.

"Juni, I really don't think . . ."

"It's OK." She looks back at him, calm and composed. "Just give me a minute. I want to try something."

She faces the door again and closes her eyes. Raises her right hand and holds her palm up to the open doorway. I nudge up beside Dervish, wondering what she's doing. He's staring at her uncertainly.

Juni takes a breath. Holds it. Murmurs something softly. The light in the room dims and her fingers glow. Then the lights come back up strong again and the glow in her fingers fades.

She steps forward into the study and nothing happens.

Dervish stands outside, gaping at her as she does a twirl and smiles at him. "You . . . the magic . . . the spells . . . you lifted them!"

Juni snaps her fingers. A book shoots off a shelf and into her hand. "Tah-dah!" she sings, like when I first met her at school. Then she looks at Dervish seriously. "I've had a busier year than I let you know," she says.

Then Dervish is through the door, by her side, babbling with excitement, asking about her magical abilities, what she can do, who taught her. A dozen questions a second, Juni laughing and shaking her head, struggling to answer them all.

I linger outside, staring with disbelief at my uncle and Juni Swan, bewildered and, for some reason I can't put my finger on, oddly uneasy.

A FAMILIAR FACE

✠   ✠   ✠

IT'S official — Dervish Grady luvs Juni Swan!

It's only been a week since she turned up at the mansion, but she's seen more of my uncle in that time than I've seen of him in three months. She spent most of last weekend at our place, four of the nights since, and they're getting together this weekend too.

They talk about magic a lot. Juni is able to channel magical energy when it's in the air around her. She tapped into her power in Slawter. She wanted to discuss it with Dervish and learn how to hone her talents, but she wasn't ready to face him. So she made inquiries, found others who are part of that magical underworld, and studied with them in her spare time while she was putting her professional life back together. She advanced quickly and has blossomed into a powerful mage over the past few months.

Dervish is gaga over her. He was attracted to her in *Slawter* and has thought of her a lot since then. But his feelings have gone over the moon since she came back and he found out they had so much in common — most importantly, magic. He's so dazzled by her, it's unreal. I think if she asked him to get on his bike and ride to the other side of the world, he would.

I'm a little dazed by it all. From being a vague friend and temporary school counselor, Juni's become a central part of my life. I feel like a tornado has struck and nothing will ever be the same again. I was used to having just Dervish around the house. It got to feel natural. Now that's changed faster than I would have believed possible. I can't get my head around it.

But I'll have to, because these two are just warming up. I came down for breakfast this morning and found Dervish and Juni already in the kitchen, making out, and I swear if he'd had his tongue any farther down her throat he'd have been licking her lungs!

✠ Bill-E thinks the Dervish-Juni match is great. We've been spending more time together since Loch's death, hanging out at lunch, having long chats like in the old days. I thought he might be jealous of all the time Juni spends with Dervish but he's not bothered.

"It's what Dervish needs," he contends. "He's been alone too long."

"He had me," I huff.

"It's not the same thing." Bill-E laughs. "It'll be good for him. Maybe he'll get out more and stop moping around the place."

"Dervish doesn't mope."

"Yes, he does," Bill-E insists. "At least he did until Juni came along."

✠ Juni knows I've been thrown by the recent developments. She hasn't mentioned her relationship with Dervish or how her moving in might affect me. But she's asked several times, at home and in our sessions, if there's anything I want to talk about apart from Loch's death, if anything else is bothering me. Each time I've said no and glanced away. She hasn't pressed it. Giving me time. Leaving me alone until I'm ready to discuss it with her willingly.

✠ In the middle of all the confusion, Reni comes back to school.

I don't know what to say when we first come face-to-face. Apart from at the funeral, when we didn't speak, I haven't seen her since Loch's death. My first reaction — a huge bolt of guilt. I covered up the truth about the accident, helped move the body, lied to protect Dervish's secret.

Several seconds of horrible silence. Then, "Hi," Reni whispers.

"Hi," I croak.

She leans towards me and rests her face on my chest. "I miss him, Grubbs," she says, voice cracking.

"Me too," I moan.

Floods of tears. Both of us.

It's easier after that. Not the same as before — it never will be — but it's OK, especially when we're with the others. Now everyone talks openly about Loch, the accident, how hard it's been, not shying away from the subject. We have Juni to thank for that. She's had all of us in her office or visited us at home since she came, working doggedly to help us talk about and deal with our grief. Life for us would be a hell of a lot harder without her.

✤ "What are you doing this weekend?" Shannon asks Reni on Friday.

"Nothing much," Reni says. "Staying in. Studying. I have a lot to catch up on."

"Scratch that," Shannon snorts. "You're coming to the movies with the rest of us. I won't take no for an answer. Grubbs, you're coming too."

"Yes, boss." I grin, glad for an excuse to get out of the house. Juni's not very big, but the place feels crowded when she's around.

"How will we get there?" Reni asks. There's a small theater in the Vale but we hardly ever go to it. Much more fun going to a multiplex in one of the bigger nearby towns.

"Frank's Dad will take us," Shannon says. Frank's father is a taxi driver and owns a van. "Won't he, Frank?" Shannon flutters her eyelids at him, buttering him up.

"I'll see what I can do," Frank mutters.

"Can Bill-E come?" I ask, eager to involve him.

"Sure," Shannon says after a moment's hesitation. "The more the merrier."

The gang's been nice about Bill-E since the accident. They don't mind me including him in our lunchtime talks and after-school activities. But I can feel the mood shifting back to the way it used to be. Bill-E's not one of us, and though he was temporarily accepted due to the exceptional circumstances, the natural order of the school world must soon be resumed. The day's fast arriving when I'll have to make a choice — Bill-E or the others.

But that's a bridge to cross another time. This weekend's about friends, films, and fun. The more serious stuff can wait.

✠ Dervish and Juni spend the night practicing magic. It seems that Juni has quite a gift. She's learned a lot over the past few months and can run rings around many of my uncle's spells.

"Have you asked her to join the Disciples?" I inquired earlier this evening, half joking, half serious. "You could go on demon-bashing weekends together, maybe check out some punk concerts at the same time."

"I don't know," Dervish muttered, not picking up on the joke. "I really don't want to involve her. That life's so dangerous. But I can't stand by and let such power go to waste. We need all the mages we can get. And I think she'll want to join. That might even be why she came looking for me — personal feelings aside, she's seen the Demonata in action and learned about the Disciples when they came to Slawter to clean up. She knows what the world's up against, the war that's being fought. Maybe she wants to help. I'll have to broach the subject soon but I'm not looking forward to it."

As wrapped up as he is with Juni, Dervish hasn't forgotten about me. He still checks on me most nights, monitoring me, quizzing me about what I'm feeling, worried about what might lie ahead. We're halfway through the lunar month. I'm just a couple of weeks away from the insanity again. Dervish isn't treating it lightly. For all the time he's spent with Juni and all the excitement and hope he's experiencing, he hasn't neglected his obligations to me. He's been in contact with everyone he can think of, trying to find out more about my situation, if anyone's heard of anything like it before. Working hard for my benefit.

He hasn't mentioned the Lambs but I'm sure he's thinking about them, just as I am, every night, unable to turn away from the thoughts of what must be done if the beast emerges and I change.

✚ Heading out to the movies. I stick my head into the study, to let Dervish and Juni know I'm going. They're sitting together on the floor, facing each other, fingers joined, eyes closed, breathing deeply. Working on a spell. They don't hear me when I call.

I walk in and scribble down a note. As I'm sticking it to the front of Dervish's PC, my glance slides to where Juni's sitting. I can see her eyes glowing behind her eyelids. She looks creepy. I leave quickly and race down the stairs, not sure what it was that freaked me so much, only knowing that I'm glad to be putting some space between us.

✚ Eating in a 1950s-style diner before the movie. Everyone excited and buzzing, except me. I keep thinking about Juni's eyes, trying to pinpoint what it was about them that unnerved me.

Bill-E's excited to be with us, though he finds it hard to join in all the talk. He'll start to say something, then stop and think about the best way to phrase it. By the time he has the words straight inside his head, the topic's changed. If he'd just be himself he'd be fine. But he thinks he has to be extra witty and cool around us, and by worrying and hesitating, he comes across as dumb and stumbling. I think about saying something to him but then I start thinking about Juni's eyes again.

Reni sits beside me for the movie. After a while she takes my hand. I half turn to smile at her and she smiles back. I thought Loch's death might drive a wedge between us but it hasn't. She still wants to be my girlfriend. Maybe it's even more important to her now than it was before — the more she focuses on me, the less she'll brood about Loch.

I start to lean over, mouth dry, spinal cord tingling.

But then I think of Juni's eyes again and it finally clicks. The glow reminded me of the fiery, eyeless sockets of one of Lord Loss's familiars — the charmless hell-baby known as Artery.

I pull away from Reni. She stares at me, surprised and slightly hurt. I force a bitter smile. "Later," I whisper. "I'm nervous, you know?" Letting her think I'm shy. Unable to tell her that thoughts of demons have set my teeth trembling, that I'm afraid I might accidentally bite her tongue if we kiss.

Reni smiles back and gives my hand a squeeze. "I know," she says, finding it sweet. She leans her head on my shoulder and sighs. "When you're ready, give me a shout. I can wait."

I lay my head on hers and close my eyes, drowning out the sounds of the movie, trying to listen to her heartbeat, feeling her hair soft against my cheek — but not able to stop thinking about Juni's eyes and demons.

✤ ✤ ✤

✤ As we come out of the theater I spot a homeless guy sitting by the side of one of the mall's water fountains. We're a long way off but he looks like the same one I ran into on the path home last week. As the others go to the restaurant again, for milk shakes, I stop and fix my gaze on the bum. I'm certain it's him — same shaggy beard, long hair, old clothes, bunch of flowers in a buttonhole. And maybe it's my imagination, but he seems to be looking back at me, returning my stare.

I start toward him, not entirely sure why but bothered by his being here, wanting to make sure it's the same man. Then Reni notices I'm not with the group. She calls my name. When I don't respond, she calls again, sharply.

"Sorry," I mutter, taking my eyes off the bum. "Thought I saw someone I knew."

"Who?" Reni asks.

"Nobody." I smile when she frowns at me. "A teacher. But it wasn't. Come on, let's go order our shakes."

"You're in a strange mood tonight," Reni comments, towing me along to catch up with the others.

Just before we turn the corner, I look back at the fountain. But nobody's there now. The bum has gone.

✤ Home. Troubled. Thinking about the bum. Probably nothing, just coincidence that I've seen him a couple of times. But it might be something more. We're protected here from demons, Dervish has said it dozens of times. But some demons have human assistants. What if the homeless man is working for Lord Loss, waiting for the chance to knock me out and cart me away to a place where the demon master can set his evil hands on me?

I decide to tell Dervish. I might wind up looking like a frightened idiot, jumping at shadows, but it's best not to take chances with stuff like this. I look for Dervish in his study, then his bedroom, but I only find Juni, sitting on the edge of Dervish's bed, staring out the window, pensive.

"Hi," I say. "Is Dervish around?"

"He's gone for Chinese."

"Oh." The local Chinese restaurant does home deliveries, but Dervish doesn't trust them to send the correct food. He always picks it up himself. "No worries. I'll catch him when he's back." I start to leave.

"Grubbs," Juni stops me. She pats the space on the bed next to her. There's a long silence as I sit beside her. She continues to stare out the window. She's so thin, I feel even bigger than normal sitting next to her.

"I saw you earlier, in the study," Juni says.

"How?" I frown. "Your eyes were closed."

"I could see through the lids — part of the spell. You looked scared. You ran away as if I frightened you." I fidget uncomfortably. "Are you afraid that Dervish is falling in love with me? That I'm going to steal his love for you?"

"No," I laugh. "That wasn't it at all."

"Then why did you look so spooked?"

"Your eyes." I clear my throat. "They were like a demon's that I fought."

Juni tenses when I mention the *D* word. Then relaxes.

"We haven't talked much about that, have we?" she notes softly.

"No."

"I'm still haunted by what happened," she whispers. "I'm dealing with it, but it's hard. Knowing there are demons in the world . . . or tearing at the edges of it . . . wanting to grab us and destroy . . ."

"I know exactly how you feel. I hate them too. They terrify me." I blush at the confession. "That's why I ran. I didn't realize it till later, but your eyes reminded me of a demon's. I panicked. It was silly, but . . ." I shrug.

"You think I have a demon's eyes?" Juni asks, bemused.

"No." I chuckle. "It was just magic. Dervish told me magic comes from demons, that the energy we tap into has seeped through from the Demonata's universe. Every time we cast a spell, we use a bit of demonic energy. I guess it makes us look like them sometimes. This was just the first time I noticed it."

Juni nods, understanding. Then, out of nowhere, she says, "Dervish is going to ask me to move in."

"Oh?" I blink.

"I don't know if I should." She looks worried. "This has taken me by complete surprise. Maybe I need to slow things down. Stay away for a while. Give us all some space and time."

I stare at her clumsily. I can't think of anything to say. I know nothing about stuff like this. After a few seconds, Juni laughs and lays a hand on my knee. "Sorry. I don't expect you to decide for me. I just needed to say it out loud."

"I . . . I think . . . I mean . . . Dervish likes you. *Really* likes you. I . . . I think you should say yes."

"You wouldn't mind?" she asks softly.

"No."

"You're sure?" Her fingers tighten on my knee. "Since I got involved with Dervish, I've noticed a change in your response to me. I wasn't sure if you approved of our relationship. I thought you didn't like me, that you didn't want me to —"

"No," I interrupt. "That's crazy. I . . . No." Smiling now. "It's been strange, having you here, but I'm not against it. Honest. I'd like it if you moved in."

Juni smiles blazingly. "You don't know how glad I am to hear that." She leans over and kisses my cheek. My blush darkens and spreads. She tweaks my nose, then gets up. "Come on," she says, heading for the door. "Dervish will be back soon. We ordered extra in case you wanted some. You can help me set the table."

Following her down the stairs, grinning to myself, delighted to find that I truly don't mind if she comes to live with us. Figuring crowded might not be such a bad thing for this hollow old house.

✤ Late Sunday. Juni was right. Dervish asked her last night if she'd come live with us. She agreed, but said it would have to be for a trial period. They'll see how they get on and if things don't work, she'll move out again.

She made the big move today. Didn't have much to bring. She's moved around a lot this year, living out of a suitcase. She had a house once, but sold it when she accepted the movie job with Davida Haym. She's been living in hotels since then. Says she has bits and pieces in storage, which she can get later, but there's no rush.

Dervish is like a child at Christmas. When Juni left to check out of her hotel this morning, he spent the time polishing and cleaning, making sure everything would be shiny and perfect when she returned. He's been dancing around the house like a pantomime figure, whistling, sometimes singing out loud.

Give me a break!

They're in bed now. It's nearly two in the morning. They've probably been asleep for hours but I can't close my eyes. Worrying about lycanthropy. Magic. Juni moving in and how that's going to change things. Loch. Reni. The bum. (I forgot to tell Dervish about him.)

I get up and dress. Pad downstairs and let myself out. Start walking, then jogging. Soon I'm running, breathing hard, breath turning to mist on the cool night air. I develop a stitch. Ignoring it, I run until it feels as if my stomach is on fire. Finally I stop and bend over, panting like a thirsty dog. When I can breathe normally I set off again, but only jogging this time, pacing myself.

It's hard to jog at night. The forest is dark around me. Have to be careful where I put my feet. But I'm not afraid. The sounds and smells of the night don't scare me. I'm safe here, on home turf.

I jog without direction, simply enjoying the exercise. Letting my feet guide me. Not keeping track of my route, confident I can find my way back.

Then I round a patch of briars and see scatterings of rocks

and dirt — I'm at the entrance to the cave. I stop and squint suspiciously. Dervish hasn't had time to fill in the hole. He stuck a crate down it and covered it with soil and small stones, so nobody would fall down into the cave, but that's as far as he got.

I approach the hole cautiously, wondering if I've been drawn here by some external force or if it's just coincidence. I listen closely for whispers but I can't hear anything. Can't sense anything either — no magical warmth within, or feeling that I'm being summoned.

I stop at the edge of the hole and stare down into darkness, thinking about Loch. It seems so long ago that we were messing around here, dreaming of Lord Sheftree's buried treasure. Everything was simple then. You don't recognize the good times in life until it all goes bad and you look back and see how lucky you were, how easy you had things.

I wonder where Loch is now, if there's an afterlife, what it's like if there is. Is he sitting on a cloud, plucking at the strings of a harp? Wrestling with angels? Being waited upon by beautiful women? Does he know the answers to all the questions in the universe? Has he come back as somebody else or as an animal? Or is there nothing when you die? I know people have souls, but do they vanish into oblivion when the body shuts down? Is life the start and finish of all that we are? Is Loch —

"You're out late."

A voice behind me. I whirl and spot the bum, half hidden by shadows, watching me with a little smile that's hard to see behind the tangled bush of his beard.

"Who are you?" I shout. "Why are you following me?"

The man steps forward and I get my first good look at him. Dark skin, but I think the color has more to do with dirt than with flesh pigment. Black hair streaked with patches of grey and white. Small build. Cracked fingernails, but not caked with dirt as you'd expect — clean as a surgeon's. Small eyes, blue or grey.

"You should be asleep," the bum says. A deep voice. Hard to place the accent.

"Who are you?" I growl again, looking for something to defend myself with.

The bum walks past me, to the edge of the hole. Stares down, the same way I was staring moments before. "A grave fit for a king," he murmurs, then looks at me and smiles crookedly. "Have anyone in mind for it?"

"Who are you?" I ask for the third time, but my voice is trembling now. This is no ordinary bum. There's something powerful and dangerous about him.

The bum doesn't answer my question. Instead he looks up at the sky — at the *moon.* "Won't be long now," he says casually, then skirts the hole and walks off, not looking back, disappearing into the cover of the forest within seconds.

I stay where I am for a minute, shivering. Then bolt for home, to wake Dervish — the hell with his beauty sleep — and tell him about the mysterious, ominous stranger.

✠ Almost back at the mansion, ready to scream myself hoarse about the bum, when I slow down, frown, and pause.

Maybe Dervish already knows.

The bum knew who I was. I'm pretty sure he knew about the cave, too, and what happened there. And he definitely knew about the moon and what it's doing to me — that was clear by his mocking tone. If he is a servant of Lord Loss, that would have been the perfect place to ambush me. I was alone. I didn't know he was there until he spoke. He could have clubbed me over the head or injected me with a sleeping drug. But he didn't. So I doubt he's in league with the demon master. If that's the case, he could only have known all those things if he'd been told. And Dervish is the only one who could have told him.

Flashback. Dervish's study . . . him on the phone . . . checking afterward . . . finding the black folder with the numbers and names.

Figuring — the bum must be one of the Lambs. A scout, sent to keep an eye on me. Dervish promised to summon a magician to help, but instead he called in the Lambs, to be safe, in case I turn and he can't handle me alone. The bum has been shadowing me ever since, ready to move quickly if need be.

I enter the house and creep up the stairs. I don't wake Dervish or ask him about the bum. Just undress and crawl into bed. Cold. Stiff. Terrified. *Alone.*

A SECRET SHARED

✠ ✠ ✠

EVERYTHING'S a blur. School, chatting with my friends, playing happy family with Dervish and Juni. Life goes on as normal around me, and I take part, the way I always have. But I'm not fully there. Always thinking about the moon, the cave, the bum, Dervish (*possibly*) scheming behind my back. Waiting for the change to hit. Going to bed tense every night, lying in the dark, wondering if this is when I'll turn. Stiffening whenever one of my fingers twitches or my stomach growls. Terror when my lips lift back over my teeth in a wolflike snarl — then relief when I realize I'm only yawning.

I discuss some of it with Dervish but I'm reluctant to share everything. The more I think about it, the more positive I am — he called in the Lambs. I resent him for that. There's no real reason to. It's not like he's washing his hands of me. I'm sure he'll be extra careful, that he won't let them act unless I'm beyond saving. But why summon them so soon? He didn't with Bill-E. He kept them in the dark.

Dealt with it himself while there was still hope. I was sure he'd act the same way with me.

Of course, I'm different. We can't work the Lord Loss angle anymore. Dervish didn't call the Lambs in last time because he planned to fight for Bill-E's humanity. If he won, Lord Loss would have cured Bill-E. If he lost, they'd have both been slaughtered by the demon master. Either way, no need for the Lambs. I'm not that lucky. There's no escape clause in my case.

Also, there's the magic. Dervish can deal with a werewolf but perhaps not one with magical powers. Maybe he's scared, isn't sure what I'll be capable of when I turn, doesn't feel he can handle me solo, wants the security of backup. Perfectly logical if he does. I can't blame him for that.

But even so, I feel betrayed and the feeling won't go away. I should talk with him, tell him I know he called in the Lambs, discuss my disappointment, give him the chance to explain.

But I don't. Afraid to bring the subject out into the open, like when I first became aware of the magic inside me and kept it secret. Ludicrously hoping that I'm wrong about the bum, that things aren't at such an advanced stage, that I can still be saved. Figuring if I don't talk about it, maybe it will go away.

Grubbs Grady — human ostrich!

✠ A week to go.

Today, at lunch, when we're alone, Reni asks if anything is wrong. I haven't been paying her the kind of attention she expects. She wants to know if I've lost interest, if I'm seeing or thinking about somebody else. She puts it lightly, tries to make a joke of it, but I can see the suspicion and hurt in her eyes.

I lie. Say things are the same as always. Make excuses. Tell her there's a lot of confusion in my life — Loch dying (not that I put it so bluntly), Juni moving in with Dervish. I even mention exams and the future, pretending I'm worried about the direction I'm taking.

She buys it. Thinks I'm going through a midteen crisis, that it has nothing to do with her. Willing to wait for my mood to improve. Confident I'll be back looking to put the moves on her once I sort through my problems. Never guessing that they might be the ripping-her-throat-open-with-my-teeth type of moves — if I turn into a werewolf next weekend.

✚ Walking home slowly, watching for the bum. I've caught glimpses of him since that night at the cave, hanging around school, on the streets of Carcery Vale, once in the trees across from my bedroom window. But he's kept at a safe distance. No follow-up contact. Slips away if I try to approach.

I'm surprised he even spoke to me that once. Maybe it was an accident — late at night, standing guard in the forest, at the scene of a tragedy. Perhaps the mood affected him and he spoke without meaning to. I'm sure even the executioners of the Lambs are prone to human slipups every now and then.

Thinking about the bum and the Lambs as I let myself in. Wondering how they kill the werewolves. I imagine it's clinical and undramatic, probably a powerful poison, injected humanely. But I can't help playing out shock-horror scenes — hordes of Lambs dressed as bums surrounding me, attacking me with machetes and clubs, a slow, humiliating, painful death.

"Grubbs," Dervish calls as I'm heading up the stairs, disrupting my train of morbid thoughts. "Could you come see me when you're ready?"

"Sure." Up to my room. Toss my bag into a corner. Out of my uniform swiftly, into jeans and a baggy sweater seconds later. Jog back down in my socks to find Dervish and Juni sitting on one of the couches in the TV room, looking edgy and stern.

I take a seat, wary. I look at them and they stare at me. A long, ragged silence. Then Dervish speaks quickly. "I've told Juni about you. About *us*. The family curse. What's been happening with you recently."

I blink slowly and glance at Juni. Can't tell what she's thinking. Wearing her most enigmatic counselor's face.

"I thought long and hard about this," Dervish says, leaning forward. "It would have been easy to ask Juni to go away next weekend and keep her out of the loop. Easy and safe." He looks at her. She smiles briefly and lays a hand on his. "But we need her help. I don't know why, but you've stopped talking to me. This past week or two, you've been withdrawn, moody, sullen. Maybe it's just fear. But I think there's more to it. You've cut me out as if you have issues with me, and that's not good. I need to know what you're thinking and feeling. I can't help you if I don't know what's going on inside your head."

"You think Juni can open me up," I say stiffly. "Stick me on a couch, get into my brain, worm out the truth."

"Maybe," Dervish mutters.

"We only have your best interests at heart," Juni says. "This is a difficult time for you. Dervish wants to help. I do too. If you have problems with your uncle — or with me — you should get them out in the open. Or, if it's something you don't want to discuss with Dervish, perhaps you can tell me in private."

"Patient to counselor?" I sneer.

"If you like," she says calmly. "I'd rather talk informally as a friend, but if you prefer we can do it professionally, with the guarantee of confidentiality."

"I don't mind," Dervish says. "I just want to help you survive the next week. If I've upset you and you don't want to tell me about it, fine. But you don't have to cut Juni out. Surely you can talk with her if not with me."

"What if there's no problem?" I mumble. "What if I'm just scared to death that I'm going to turn into a werewolf and don't feel like talking about it?"

"That would be entirely understandable," Juni says. "But unless you're sure that's the case, you should discuss it with someone. Talking about your fears can be a highly positive experience. You know that, Grubbs. You're not an innocent child. Going through this alone is a bad call."

"Especially as you might not even be going through it," Dervish says. I look at him with a raised eyebrow. "You might not be turning. Juni thinks . . ." He stops and looks at her.

"Just because people in your family are victims of a disease that alters their bodies — I refuse to refer to them as were-wolves, since that's a hysterical term — it doesn't mean *you* are going to change," Juni says. "From what you've described, it sounds as if you're in trouble, but it's by no means certain. This might be a mental problem, not a physical one."

"You think I'm imagining things?" I growl.

"Perhaps," Juni says. "The mind can play tricks on the most ordinary people — and you're far from ordinary! To come through what you have . . . to see so much of the world — and other worlds — at such a young age . . . to lose your loved ones in a grisly fashion, then fight for your brother's life . . . what happened to us in Slawter . . . Your resilience amazes me. You're one of the strongest people I've ever met, and I'm not saying that to stroke your ego. You're incredible, Grubbs."

I smile crookedly, blushing, tears coming to my eyes. Part of me wants to leap up and hug her. Another part wants me to wave her compliment away and act cool. In the end I just carry on smiling, blushing, and crying lightly.

"But even the strongest of us has a breaking point," Juni says. "Maybe Loch was yours. Or perhaps there's something else, a small upset you're not even aware of. It's possible you're turning — but it's also possible you're not. I want to try to find out. In a week we'll know for sure. But we can cover a lot of ground in a week. It could make a real difference if you're wrong about the change."

"And if I'm right?" I ask tightly.

Juni beams. "We'll just have to fire a silver bullet through the middle of your forehead."

I laugh loudly. Dervish does too.

"My sense of humor's rubbing off on her." Dervish chuckles proudly.

"You say that like it's a good thing."

"Boys, boys," Juni tuts. "Let's not get sidetracked. Grubbs, will you accept my offer to help? Talk with me privately if you have something you don't want to say to both of us? Accept me as a counselor if not a friend?"

I almost blurt it out and tell them I know about the Lambs, which is why I've been so surly. But that would mean a confrontation with Dervish, admitting to his face that I feel like he betrayed me. I can't do that, not after all the good things he's done for me. If I'm wrong, it would hurt him to hear me speak that way.

So I take Juni up on her offer, lower my head to hide my thoughts, and mutter, "Yeah, talking with you sounds good."

"Thank you," Juni says.

"Nice one," Dervish adds.

And we pretend for a while that everything's fine and all our problems have been solved.

✠ Long talks with Juni at school in the day and at home in the evenings. Not just about Loch. We cover all kinds of ground — my past, parents, Gret, Lord Loss, the institute, life with Dervish, Bill-E changing into a werewolf, *Slawter.* All the things we didn't discuss before, when she was only interested in helping me deal with Loch's death.

We spend a lot of time on magic, the buzz of energy I sometimes feel in my gut, what I've done with it, my mind-set when the magic was flowing through me. With Dervish's permission, Juni runs some tests, trying to tap into my magical core, to find out what's going on inside, what I might be capable of doing. But she comes up blank. If the magic's still there, it's buried too deep for her to find.

She also spends a lot of time researching the Demonata, pumping Dervish for information, finding out all she can about them. She's especially hot on Lord Loss — if he's able to cure our lycanthropic curse, she doesn't see why we shouldn't be able to do it too.

"We're not powerful enough," Dervish tells her.

"Maybe it's just a matter of knowing the right spells," Juni suggests.

"I don't think so," he says. "If that was the case, Bartholomew Garadex would have discovered them. He was dogged in his determination to end the curse, but he got nowhere by himself. It takes a demon master to overturn the spell."

"But —"

"No," Dervish insists. "Bartholomew was the world's most powerful magician of the past couple of centuries. If he wasn't able to do it, none of us can. We'd be wasting our time if we went down that path."

"What if we tried Lord Loss?" she asks. "Maybe you're wrong about him not accepting the chess challenge again."

"No." Dervish laughs shortly. "That isn't an option."

"But if he's the only one who can turn Grubbs back . . ." Juni persists.

"It's not an option," Dervish says again. Firmly. End of discussion.

✚ ✚ ✚

✠ I'm enjoying my time alone with Juni. She's different than when she was merely counseling me. Magic is her thing, what really interests her. She's more open when we're talking about spells and demons. She lets her guard down and stops treating me like a patient. Sometimes it seems we talk more about her and magic than we do about me and my problems, but that's fine.

She still sees Bill-E and some of my friends in her professional capacity, but not as much as before. Her last day at our school is at the end of the week. Misery's not returning but he's being replaced by another counselor. Juni's done what she set out to. Time to move on to another job, another challenge. But she's not thinking about that until after the weekend. First she wants to see what happens to me when the full moon rises.

✠ Thursday. Testing for magical potential again. In the TV room. Dervish is in the kitchen, keeping out of the way. Juni's trying something new. Up to this point she's probed carefully, gently, just scratching the surface. Tonight she wants to go deeper.

"Relax," she says, standing behind me as I squat on a stool. "Clear your mind." She puts her hands on my head. "I'm going to provoke you." Her fingers slide to my neck and her nails scratch the flesh there, lightly. "I'm going to pick and poke at your flesh while I jab magically at you. It will be more irritating that way. I'm hoping something will stir within you in response, drive me out, and stop me from hurting you."

"Hurting?" I repeat uneasily.

"Don't worry." I sense her smile. "I won't really hurt you. Trust me."

She massages my shoulders. At first it's nice but then she digs her thumbs in. Works her way down my arms, pinching, scratching. Nothing too severe. Just irritating, like she said.

She mutters spells while she works. I feel magic seep into me, a weird sensation beneath my skin. It's like having my leg fall asleep, only I'm itchy all over.

Minutes pass. Juni works. Down my back, my chest, my legs. Very prickly now, twitching and jerking, wishing she'd stop, wondering if I should say something or just grit my teeth and bear it. Finally, when I'm on the point of calling it quits, she releases me.

"Nothing," she says, sounding disappointed. She puts a couple of fingers on my left cheek. "You can open your eyes."

As I blink my eyes open, I catch her looking at me. A strange look. As if she thinks I'm lying and disapproves of me. There's even a shade of hostility in it.

"It was definitely there before," I tell her as she takes her fingers away.

"I'm sure it was," she says, the suspicious look disappearing.

"Maybe it'll come back tomorrow or the next night. When the moon . . ." I nod towards the window, where the curtains keep out the light of the almost full globe.

"Perhaps," she says. "Magic is certainly affected by lunar movements. Most mages experience a surge of extra energy around the time of a full moon. But it's strange for you not to be showing *any* signs."

She sits beside me. Brings a hand up and ruffles my hair. Smiles fondly, then whispers, "Tell me your secret. The thing you won't talk to Dervish about. I haven't asked before and I won't ask again if you don't answer. But I think you want to tell someone."

Mouth dry. Heart beating hard. I wasn't going to tell her. I meant to keep it secret. But now that she's asked, I realize she's right. I want to share it with her. Hell, I'm suddenly longing to spill the beans.

"He called the Lambs," I croak.

"Lambs?" she frowns. "What do sheep have to do with this?"

"No. Family executioners. The Lambs. When one of us turns . . . if the parents can't bear to keep them alive, but can't kill them by themselves, the Lambs do it."

"Ah. I remember. The dream in Slawter. Their laboratory." Her frown deepens. "You think Dervish summoned them? That he's plotting against you?"

"Not plotting," I mutter. "But if I turn and he can't control me, I think he wants them to kill me. He said he was going to ask a magician for help, but he didn't. He called in the Lambs instead. And that's . . . y'know . . . not *fine*, but I know why he did it. I just wish he'd waited. Or told me he was summoning them."

"He hasn't told you?"

"No."

"Then how do you know?"

I explain about his conversation on the phone, the black folder, the bum. She asks me to describe the bum but I can only give her a very general description.

"You're certain he's a Lamb?" she asks dubiously.

"Pretty sure."

"He never said?"

"No. But he's been hounding me. I've seen him outside this house. And at the cave." We've told her about the cave, how Loch really died. Dervish took her there to get a sense of it. One magical whiff of the place and she agreed he'd done the right thing, that it needed to be hidden from the world. "Why would he be following me if he wasn't one of the Lambs?" I ask.

"There are all sorts of people in the world," Juni says. "Some follow boys for dark — but very human — reasons."

"I know." I shift uncomfortably. "But it'd be an awful coincidence, this bum taking an interest in me at this precise time."

"I sometimes think the world runs on coincidences." Juni pats my hand. "Don't worry about the homeless man. I'll keep an eye out for him. And I'll do a bit of work on Dervish and find out if he really contacted the Lambs."

"You won't tell him what I said, will you?" I ask, alarmed, not wanting him to think I've been bad-mouthing him behind his back.

"I'll be discreet," Juni vows, and gets up to leave.

"Juni," I stop her. "When you find out . . . if he *did* call them in . . . will you tell me the truth?"

A long pause. Then, "Do you really want to know?"

"Yes."

"You can handle it if he did?"

"Yes."

She smiles and touches my cheek again. "You're so brave," she whispers, then draws the fingers away. "I'll tell you what I find out. I promise. No lies. You can always trust me, Grubbs, about everything — even if you can't trust Dervish."

SHAKE, DOG, SHAKE

✠   ✠   ✠

THE shakes. *Bad.* Dervish and Juni keep me pressed down on the bed, talking constantly, wiping sweat from my face with a series of fresh towels, Juni muttering calming spells that don't make the slightest difference.

Friday. The night before the full moon. The sickness struck at school, in the middle of physics. I had to rush for the bathroom. Didn't make it. Was violently sick against the classroom door. Lots of cheers from the boys, gasps of disgust from the girls. Didn't stop to catch an earful from Mr. Clifford. Bolted for the boys' room and spent the next ten minutes hugging a hard plastic seat.

Juni drove me home. I threw up twice into a bag along the way. I've had the dry heaves since then, though Juni makes me drink lots of water, so sometimes I vomit clear, acidic liquid.

"You're going to be OK," Dervish lies, grasping my shoulders as I cry out in pain. It feels as if there's a second body growing within mine, forcing its way out.

"I could try a sleeping spell," Juni says.

"Don't be stupid," Dervish barks. "The only reason he hasn't turned is because he's fighting so damn hard. He can't fight if he's asleep."

"Sorry. I wasn't thinking. I just hate to see him in so much agony."

I scream hoarsely, sure my head is about to split down the middle. Dimly aware of a heat in my stomach, the magical heat that was there last month. It's battling the wolfen change, keeping me human, denying the demands of the beast. Unable to tell Dervish and Juni about it. Incapable of speech. Only screams.

✛ Later. The moon starting to dip. Moments of quiet after hours of madness. The sheets of the bed are ripped in many places. Dervish is cut above his left eye and both his cheeks are bruised.

"Did . . . I do . . . that?" I groan.

"No," he deadpans, carefully pouring water down my throat. "I walked into a door."

"We thought we'd lost you," Juni says, squeezing my hand. I've scratched her forehead but it's not a deep cut.

"The . . . magic," I gasp. Both of them pause. "Did you . . . feel it?"

"No," Dervish says.

"It was . . . there. That's how . . . I fought. Would have . . . turned . . . otherwise."

"Juni?" Dervish asks.

"I sensed *something*," she says hesitantly. "I wasn't sure if it was magic or the energy generated by the . . . the alteration."

"The werewolf," I grin weakly. "Go on, say it, just once."

"There's no such creature," Juni huffs.

I start to reply but pain strikes again, deep in my gut. I double over. The water comes up almost as quickly as it went down. Hits Dervish hot in the face. He ignores it and pins me to the bed, talking fast again, trying to comfort me, his words only a dim murmur above my endless, wretched screams.

✤ The beast snarls and claws at my skin from the inside. It can't speak — it's a wild animal — but I can sense its feelings and translate them into words. *Release me*, it would demand if it could. *End the pain. Set me free. Become what you must. We can run as one and take the night.*

"No!" I howl back, clubbing it down with fists of a magic I don't understand.

You can't deny me.

"Get stuffed!" is my eloquent response.

The internal battle rages on but I have the sense that I'm winning. The pull of the moon is fading. The creature has lost the fight. But there's another night to come and it will be stronger then. Maybe too strong.

You can't deny me, the beast hisses again from somewhere deep inside me, deeper than it should be. *This is what we are. It's our fate.*

"I'll choose my own fate," I mutter, staying on guard, ready to fight again if it launches a last-minute attack. But it doesn't. The sun is rising. The moon's losing its luster. I've won — for now.

✠ ✠ ✠

✠ Wearily sitting up. Dervish and Juni regard me suspiciously. Both exhausted. Cut, bruised, and scratched in many places.

"What happened to you two?" I quip.

"Now he gets cocky," Dervish growls. "For the past eight or nine hours it's been screams and agony, hell on Earth. But now, with the sun rising, you feel like you can joke, regardless of the agony you've put us through."

We regard each other coolly — then laugh.

"We survived!" I shout.

"You beat it!" Dervish chortles, hugging me tight.

Juni just smiles tiredly, watching us.

When Dervish releases me, I collapse backward and stare at the ceiling.

"How do you feel?" Dervish asks. "Or is that a stupid question?"

"No," I sigh. "I don't feel so bad. Tired, but not as beat as you or Juni look. To tell the truth, I'm hungry."

"If you're expecting breakfast in bed, you're in for a nasty surprise," Juni snaps. Dervish and I giggle.

"It was strange," I mumble, recalling my battle, especially the end when I imagined the beast speaking to me. "Like I was wrestling with another person — a thing — inside myself. But *really* wrestling. Like it was there physically. My body was a ring and there were two of us inside the ropes. It was the hardest fight of my life."

"No piece of cake for us on the outside either," Dervish

says, touching his bruised cheeks. "You put us through the wringer. I know you're a colossus in the making, but I wouldn't have credited you with that much strength."

"It would have been worse if the beast had won," I tell him quietly. "I could feel it. So strong. Without the magic, it would have walked all over me, burst loose, torn into you. Tonight . . . when the moon's full . . ."

"Don't think about that. We'll take this one fight at a time. Focus on the victory now. Deal with the next bout when we're faced with it." He stands, stretches, and groans.

"Go to bed," Juni smiles. "You worked hard and took most of the blows. We both need to get a lot of sleep today, but you more than me."

"I'll be fine," Dervish says, then wobbles on his feet and almost falls. Juni steadies him, then says firmly, "Bed!"

"Yes, miss," Dervish sighs. "You coming?"

"Soon. I want to sit with Grubbs a little bit longer."

Dervish leaves, rubbing the small of his back and groaning. Juni watches him go, then examines her wounds. Murmuring spells, she brushes her fingers over the light cuts on her arms. They heal swiftly, the flesh closing neatly, only the slightest lines of red giving away the fact that she'd been scratched at all.

"Neat trick."

"A useful spell." She works on her neck and face. "It's no good on deep gashes but it's perfect for little rips like these. Better than Band-Aids. I'll fix Dervish up later."

Finishing, she turns her attention to me. Wipes my hair back from my eyes. Heals the scratch on my forehead. Rubs the flesh to make sure it's OK, then says softly, "He was terrified. I was too, but not as much as Dervish. He really loves you."

"I know."

"He'd give his life for you if it would change anything."

I stare at her silently. There are tears in her eyes. I instinctively know why she's saying this, defending him when there's no apparent need. "He called the Lambs," I whisper.

She nods miserably. "I got him to admit it. He didn't want to involve them. But if you turn, you have to be killed. He can't do that, not kill his own nephew. So, as much as he hates them . . ."

"It's OK," I tell her, forcing a weak smile. "He didn't have a choice."

"I suppose." She sighs, lowering her gaze. "I had a son once." I blink, not sure how to respond to this startling, unexpected confession. "A darling boy. He was my world. Died in his sleep a few months before his second birthday. A brain defect. There were no warning signs. Nothing anybody could have done about it."

She breaks down in tears. I pat her back clumsily, wishing I could wash her hurt away with words, feeling as useless as I've ever felt. Finally she regains control and wipes her cheeks dry.

"It almost destroyed me," she croaks. "I survived, but just barely. Became a child psychologist so I could be close to other children, ease my pain by helping them with theirs." She laughs hoarsely. "I once said you were psychologically plain. Well, I'm an open book too. Whenever anything goes wrong in my life, I hide behind my work, use it to haul myself out of whatever dark hole I've fallen into."

She takes hold of both my hands and squeezes, stronger than I imagined. "When Dervish asked me to move in, I was delighted, not just because I love him, but because it meant I could become a mother to *you*." She lets go of my left hand and strokes my cheeks, smiling warmly. "I've always wanted another son to mother but it never quite worked out until now."

The smile fades. She lets go of my other hand and stands. "I won't abandon you," she says, her voice throbbing with surprising menace. "I won't give you over to the Lambs, not unless there's no hope at all. I'll stand by you until the very, *very* end. Even if Dervish doesn't."

Then she's gone, leaving me to stare after her, jaw slack, senses whirring, not quite sure what to make of her fiercely supportive vow.

✠ A day of rest. We all sleep until early afternoon and lounge around after that. Juni's oddly distant, withdrawn and quiet. Doesn't look at me straight. Or Dervish. Almost as if she's ashamed of what she said. Or is planning something and doesn't want us to know.

✠ Evening. The shakes again. Throwing up everything I've eaten. I fight my vomitous body, sitting on the grass out back, taking the warm evening sun, determined to enjoy what might be my final sunset. Dervish and Juni are nearby. Dervish asks if I want to go in. I shake my head. Don't want to abandon the outside world. Afraid that once I do, that's it — game on . . . game over . . . doomed.

Bill-E called earlier. Wanted to come over and hang out.

Dervish made my excuses. Said I'd caught something nasty. Told Bill-E to stay away in case it was contagious. Bill-E wasn't suspicious. Why should he be?

Thinking about my brother. Wishing I'd told him about us. Dervish was right — I waited too long. I wanted to spare him the emotional roller-coaster ride of the truth but I was wrong to stall. If I change tonight and the Lambs exterminate me, he'll only think he lost a friend. He'll never know how close we really were.

I consider calling him, telling him the truth while I'm still capable of speech. But that would be lunacy. If I survive, beat this thing, or at least delay my transformation for a month, I can tell him then. Calling now would be pointless. Worse — dangerous. He might come over. Get in the way. Fall victim to the blood-crazed beast I might by that stage have become.

"Do you still have the cage?" I ask suddenly. Dervish stops talking to Juni and stares at me. "The cage in the secret cellar. Is it still there?"

He nods slowly.

"Put me in it." I thought my voice might quaver but it holds firm. I stare at him unflinchingly.

"If you start to change, we can —" he begins.

"No," I interrupt. "Do it now. Before I turn. I made a mess of you last night. I hurt Juni too. She was able to fix us up but I'll be stronger tonight. Wilder. Maybe I'll inflict damage she can't cure."

Dervish is silent. He exchanges a look with Juni.

"That could be detrimental," Juni says softly. "You believed in yourself last night. That belief gave you the strength to fight. If you allow yourself to be caged up like an animal, perhaps you'll start thinking of yourself as one. You might stop believing . . . stop fighting."

"I won't."

"It might be for the best," Dervish mutters. "If he does turn, I'm not sure we can control him."

"You have drugs," Juni says. "You can subdue him if you have to."

"Remember Meera?" I say before Dervish can answer. "When Bill-E changed, he got to her. Knocked her out before you could inject him. Almost killed her. If that happens to Juni . . ."

Dervish's jaw stiffens. "You're right. It has to be the cage." He takes Juni's hand. "It doesn't mean we're giving up. We're just being safe."

She nods reluctantly and looks at me. Her expression communicates the same thing that she promised earlier — "Trust me. I'll stand by you. Even if Dervish doesn't."

I rise quickly. "Best do it now." I take one last look at the sun. "The moon will be up soon." I put my hands on my growling stomach. "I can feel it."

✠ The cage. Howling. Screaming. Battering the bars. Dervish and Juni on the other side, roaring encouragement, telling me I'm winning, calling to the human within, the one who's rapidly disappearing, giving way to something new, deadly, beastly.

I fight but it's much harder than last night. The beast is stronger. It assaults me without pause, snapping and growling, hurling itself against the ball of magic that is my only protection, ripping into it, howling bloody murder, hell-bent on breaking free to run wild and kill.

I grip my head between my hands and scream, veins in my neck stretched, fingers curling inward into claws. I keep shouting my name, trying to hold on to my voice, but all that comes out is a jumbled snarl. And the light around me is changing, becoming darker, the shades more limited, colors fading to grey.

"Not . . . going . . . to . . . turn!" I bellow, having to fight for each word. I let go of my head. Clutch the bars of the cage. Lock gazes with Dervish, then Juni. "Not . . . going . . . to . . ." The last word becomes an inhuman shriek.

"That's right," Dervish shouts desperately. "You won't turn. You're Grubbs Grady. You'll win this fight. Gradys never lose."

"Keep fighting," Juni pleads. She puts her hands over mine. "You can do it. I know you can."

I fall away from the bars, shaking my head, roaring with pain. The beast cackles. The battle continues. Torment claims me whole.

✠ I've been fighting for hours. At least I think it's hours. Maybe it's just been minutes. Maybe I'm so far gone that I've lost track of time. Perhaps, for me, this night will last an age, never ending, an eternal fight between humanity and a force of wolfen evil.

I slump on the floor, leaning against the bars of the cage, staring around with wide, wild eyes, seeing the main desk, the key to this cage, candles, books, a chess piece in one corner, left over from my last fight here. My skin feels like it's rippling. I want to let it. I'm tired. I can't go on.

You must.

A new voice. Not my own and not the imagined voice of the beast. The voice of magic. It speaks quickly, softly, telling me we can beat this thing if we work together. It starts to explain how I can use it, the spells I need to cast, the words I must chant — but the beast picks that moment to yowl violently, filling my head with white noise, causing me to jam my hands over my ears and scream.

When the noise passes and I lower my hands, the voice of the magic is gone, or is so quiet I can't hear it. I'm not alone. I still sense it there. But I no longer feel like it can help me. I'm losing this battle. Maybe I've already lost and just don't know it yet.

✠ More fighting. Pain. Terror.

Another rare moment of rest and understanding. On the opposite side of the cage this time but in the same slumped position as before. Dervish and Juni are crouched nearby, telling me how well I'm doing, how proud they are, I'm going to win, I just have to ride it out.

I turn my head a fraction and smile sadly at Dervish. "Sorry," I croak.

"No," he snaps. "You can't give up. You have to beat this thing."

"Sorry," I mutter again, head dropping, panting hard, crying, tears hot on my cheeks, not feeling like they're mine.

"He's slipping from us," Juni says. She sounds much calmer than my uncle.

"No!" Dervish barks. "I won't let him. We have to —"

"Quiet," Juni commands.

"But we can't —"

"We won't." She reaches in and tilts my head back. It takes a few seconds but my eyes finally focus. She's studying me coolly. "He's losing concentration. We have to help him regain it. Force him back into action and spur him on to fight."

"How?" Dervish asks tightly.

"A spell. One to act on the magic within him. It will be like injecting him with adrenaline — only it's magic we'll inject into, not flesh."

"What spell?" Dervish growls. "I don't know any —"

"I've been preparing one," Juni cuts in. "Just in case." She looks away from me and trades gazes with Dervish. "It's dangerous. If it doesn't cure him, it will kill him. I didn't want to use it unless it became absolutely necessary. I still won't, not unless he slips further and concedes more ground to the . . . *werewolf*." She smiles fleetingly as she says it. Then her expression firms again. "I won't do it if you object, but I want you to know it's there if we need it. And I have to know if you'll consider letting me use it, so I can finish preparing."

Dervish looks lost, like he wants to cry. For a moment I don't think he's going to respond. But then, with a wrenching effort, he nods stiffly. "But only if there's no other choice," he wheezes.

"Of course." Juni touches his cheek lovingly. "You'll need

to go to the house. If I go ahead with the spell, there are things I'll need."

"What?"

Juni closes her eyes. A couple of seconds pass. She opens them again. "Got it?"

"Yes." Dervish laughs crazily. "You'll have to teach me how to do that." Then he stumbles for the door leading to the wine cellar.

Juni waits till he's gone, then hurries to the desk, grabs the key to the cage, and inserts it in the lock.

"What are you doing?" I mumble, backing away from her as she opens the door and enters my lair. "Get out. It's not safe. I could —"

"The Lambs are outside," Juni says, stooping beside me, taking my hands, helping me to my feet. "Dervish was in contact with them earlier. They have the house surrounded. Ready to finish you off when Dervish gives the word."

I shrug wearily. "Maybe it's for the best. I can't be helped. They —"

"No!" Juni hisses, and slaps my face. "I won't let you sacrifice yourself. I don't believe you're lost. We can get through this but only by thinking positively, only if you fight. Dervish doesn't understand. He called this wrong. He loves you but he underestimates you. He doesn't know how strong you are."

"No. I'm weak. I can't fight anymore. I just want to let it happen. Simpler that way. I'm sick of all the pain."

"I don't care how sick you are!" Juni snaps. Then her voice changes. "I'm not doing this just for you. I want you to live for *me* too."

She grabs me by the front of my sweatshirt, pulls me in close, and kisses me. It starts innocently, the way my mom used to kiss me when I was little and woke up scared in the middle of the night. But then it changes into something deeper and I kiss her back, the way I kissed Reni when we played spin the bottle.

The beast within me howls as we kiss. The magic surges and seethes. Around us the bars of the cage turn red, then crack and melt, tumbling away. The roof of the cage falls upon us. I swat it aside with a single powerful hand.

Juni releases me. She's breathing hard. "Run, Grubbs," she says, eyes bright, cheeks flushed. "Get away from the Lambs. Go the cave. Wait for me there."

"The cave? But . . . if I turn . . ."

"You won't," she vows, and kisses me again, quickly this time. *"Go!"*

Without thinking, I bolt. Leaping over the bubbling bars of the cage, I race to the other exit, the one that leads away from the house. I tear the door open and flee up the stairs. Juni cheers encouragingly behind me, then laughs, her laughter trailing me, staying with me, comforting me, urging me on.

✛ The top of the stairs. The way ahead blocked by a pair of doors, locked from the other side by chains, covered by a sheet of corrugated iron. I pause for the briefest of seconds, then set my right shoulder to the doors and thrust sharply. The chains snap. The doors explode open. The sheet of iron flies clear.

I emerge into moonlight.

Standing in the open, chest rising and falling rapidly, staring around, seeing the world with eyes one-third human, one-third animal, one-third magic. Picking out shapes, even if they're hidden from direct sight by trees or the house. Nine . . . ten . . . eleven . . . twelve. The dirty dozen. But not dirty enough to hold Grubbs Grady — überescapee!

The beast in me wants to attack, rip them open, teach them not to mess with the Grubbster. But tempting as that thought is, I push it away and break for the forest instead.

There are three members of the Lambs back here. The unexpected shattering of the doors stunned them. But they recover quickly. Their training kicks in and they move to intercept me. Large men with clubs, stun guns, nets, rifles.

"Halt!" one of them shouts, aiming a rifle. I snarl at his gun and it turns bright red. He screams and tries to throw it away. Fails, because it's burned into his flesh and welded itself to the bones in his hand.

The second Lamb rushes me, tries to bring me down with a football tackle. I grab him as he leaps, spin him around in the air, then slam him down hard, knocking him out — a perfect wrestling move. Loch would be proud. If I had time, I'd pin him for a three count. But as powerful and playful as I feel, I can't linger. If the rest of the Lambs converge, things might not go so smoothly. I think I could take them all on and beat them but it would be stupid to put myself to the test.

The third of the rear guard has fumbled out a walkie-talkie and is barking into it. I growl in his direction. Metallic claws sprout from the hard plastic and dig into the flesh and bones of the Lamb's face. Roaring with shock and pain, he tries jerking the walkie-talkie loose but the claws have dug in too deep, wiring the device to his jaw.

I leave the Lamb stumbling around, screaming, tugging at the walkie-talkie, blood pouring from his ear and cheek. I race for the cover of the trees, moving swiftly, surely, feeling more alive than ever before.

As I reach the forest I spot the bum standing nearby, watching me. I laugh at him — he saw what happened to the others and is too scared to tackle me. I think about turning his legs to jelly or setting his clothes on fire, but since he's not interfering with my escape, why bother? The spineless creep isn't worth the effort.

I want to shout, "So long, sucker!" but my vocal cords are twisted and words won't form. I settle for a mock salute instead. He stares back silently, face impassive.

Then I'm gone, sheltered from the moon and hidden from the remaining Lambs by the trees. Running with the ease of a wolf. Fast and slick, leaving no trail for anyone to follow. Heading for the cave and my reunion with Juni.

SAVAGE

✠   ✠   ✠

FOR a couple of minutes I feel like a superhuman. Legs of steel, iron lungs, running faster than any normal person ever ran, obliterating records. Where are the Olympic judges when you need them?

But then I slow. Pain sweeps through me. I stumble. The beast snarls. Writhing on the cold, hard forest floor. Sobbing. Trying to fight. I raise my head and try —

✠ Next thing I know, I'm in the hole that leads to the cave, tugging at the crate that Dervish left there, ripping it to splinters, clambering down into the dark abyss. Part of me hesitates. Grateful to still be human, eager to reach the safety of the cave, happy to wait for Juni, but remembering Dervish's warning — this cave is dangerous, a place of evil magic. Perhaps I should —

✠ In the cave. I'm howling, the howls echoing eerily. With an effort I make myself stop and the echoes die away. Then all I can hear is the waterfall and the superfast beating of my overworked heart.

How long have I been unconscious, howling, the beast thinking it had won, only for me to somehow scrap my way back and regain control? Impossible to tell but it doesn't feel like a lot of time has passed.

The dark is absolute. It scares me. The feeling of invulnerability and supremacy that drove me through the cordon of Lambs has passed. The magic's still there and so is the beast. But mostly it's just me now, human and cold, alone in the dark, thinking with horror how close I came to killing the three Lambs, hoping I didn't hurt them too much, wondering if I did the right thing by running.

I slide to the floor and pull my knees to my chest, clasping them tight, trying to see something — anything — through the darkness. Remembering Juni's kiss with confusion and shame, wondering what prompted it, or if I just imagined the adult passion. What I definitely didn't imagine — she said she'd stand by me even if Dervish gave up. She set me free and promised to meet me here.

It's wrong. Her intentions were good but we shouldn't be doing this. I should have stayed and taken what I had coming. Let Dervish handle the situation the way he thought best. He knows more about these matters than Juni or I. I've passed a fatal point. Split from Dervish. Crossed swords with the Lambs. Made a pact with Juni that's cut me off from everybody else. What if she doesn't come? What if she changes her mind and leaves me here? What if . . .

A light. I start to rise, thinking it's Juni. But then I see that it's coming from the wall of the cave, close to where the waterfall flows, just to the left of the crack I created in the rock. A strange, soft light, not natural. It comes from within the wall. Circular but jagged around the rim. And in the center, forcing its way out of the rock and into shape, the girl's face I saw when Loch died.

The jaw, cheekbones, and forehead bulge outwards, illuminated by the light. The face looks like a cross between rock and flesh, neither one nor the other but a splice of the two. When it's jutting out as far as it can — I can see the tips of its ears — the eyes open. A moment later the lips move.

She speaks with urgency, words tripping off her tongue. I can tell it's important — her need to communicate something vital is clear — but I can't understand what she's saying. The language isn't like any I've ever heard.

"I don't know what you're saying," I moan, shaking my head helplessly. In response she raises her voice and speaks even faster than before — as if *that* will help! "I can't understand you," I shout, losing my temper.

Then the pain hits again. The beast howls. Magic flares. I sink to my knees, moaning. The girl's voice rises. She yells, harassing me, repeating the same sharp phrases over and over. But I couldn't make sense of her words the first time and I can't make sense of them now. I want her to leave me alone.

"Stop," I groan, but she doesn't. "Stop." Firmer this time, glaring at her, letting her see the anger in my eyes. I need peace and quiet if I'm to fight the beast and drive it back into its den. Doesn't she realize how hard this is and that she's only making it harder?

No, she doesn't. Or if she does, she doesn't care. She keeps on jabbering, voice rising, words coming faster and faster. Then a pair of hands grow out of the rock and she points at me accusingly, at the cave in general, at the crack in the rock.

"Shut up," I hiss, feeling the beast scrape the inside of my skull with its claws. "I can't take anymore. Stop it. Stop it! *STOP!*"

With the final cry I lunge to my feet, throw my hands wide, and scream.

A sharp snapping sound — the crack beside the waterfall widens and lengthens. The girl's face and hands disappear. And the waterfall freezes. It turns to ice. A solid stretch of crystal from top to bottom, glistening beautifully, caught in full motion, an image no artist could ever hope to replicate.

I stare at the ice, mesmerized. How the hell did I do that?

Then the light where the girl's face was fades. I'm plunged into darkness again. Moments later, while my head's still spinning, I notice the glow of another light behind me. I turn, expecting the face again. But this is the flickering of a flashlight. And it's coming from overhead, from the shaft to the forest above.

"Grubbs?" someone calls — the most welcome voice in the world.

"Juni!" I cry, stumbling toward the spot where she'll enter the cave. "Come quick. You'll never believe —"

Agony. A flash of total torment. The beast, closer to the surface than ever. Incredibly powerful. The magic flares in response. The pair wrestle, spitting flames, fighting for possession of my body and soul.

I collapse, screaming. Juni shouts my name again. The world dims around me. My thoughts go thin. I try to call to warn her to stay away. But it's too late. I go under. The beast drives me down. I vanish.

✠ Returning to my senses. Indescribable relief. When I felt myself lose control that last time, I thought I was finished. No more Grubbs Grady. Lost forever. Werewolf in command from this night till doomsday. It's good — delicious! — to be back.

But relief fades as quickly as it swelled. I'm no longer in the cave. I'm in a house and there's blood everywhere. A couple of mauled, gutted bodies on the floor. Juni stands across from me, beaten and bruised, bleeding freely from her arms, head, neck. She's facing me, talking rapidly, hands outstretched and making frantic gestures, trying to calm me down.

I'm growling at her, my bloodstained fingers curled into fists, keeping her away from the corpses — apparently the beast wanted them all for himself.

I manage to stop growling and lower my hands.

"Grubbs?" Juni croaks nervously. "Is that you?"

"*Uhrs.*" I cough. Clear my throat and try again. "Yes."

"Thank god." She weeps, collapsing. "I thought you were going to kill me."

"I'd never . . ." I stop and look around. I know this house. And now that I look past the layers of blood, I know the people.

Ma and Pa Spleen!

"No!" I cry. "Not Bill-E! Tell me I didn't —"

"Behind you," Juni says through her tears.

I turn slowly, expecting the worst, ready to rip my own

heart out if I've killed my brother. But he's alive. Lying on his stomach, unconscious, bleeding from a blow to his head. But his body's moving with his breath. I go to him quickly, turn him over onto his back, make him comfortable, check that the cut to his head isn't serious.

"You changed," Juni moans. "I couldn't stop it. I thought I could tap into the magic of the cave and help. But you became a monster and tried to kill me. I managed to ward you off. Turned off the light. Hid in the darkness. Masked my smell using magic.

"Then you left. I tracked you here. You burst in before I arrived. Killed the old couple. You would have killed Billy too, but I fought and stalled you. I don't think I could have held you off much longer. If you hadn't turned back when you did . . ."

She breaks down. I stare at her, then at Bill-E. Then at the butchered Ma and Pa Spleen. I never liked them. They were cranky, selfish busybodies. Always interfering, trying to keep Bill-E and me apart. But they didn't deserve this — ripped to pieces in their own home by a savage animal of the night.

"What have I done?" I cry, sinking to the floor, burying my head in my hands. "I killed them. I'm a murderer."

"No." Juni sobs, crawling across, trying to pull my hands away. "It was the beast . . . the werewolf. You didn't do this, Grubbs. It wasn't your fault."

"Of course it was!" I scream, head shooting up. "I knew what was happening. I knew I had to be locked up, what I could do if unleashed. I should have stayed in the cage and let the Lambs slaughter me."

"Don't say that," Juni pleads.

"It's true," I cry. "*I* should be dead now, not the Spleens. It should be . . ." I stop, frowning. "But why did I come here? Why pick them and Bill-E?"

"You didn't like them," Juni reminds me.

"But I didn't hate them. And Bill-E's my best friend. Why . . . ?"

"Does it matter?" she interrupts sharply. "You were jealous of Billy or you wanted to kill his grandparents or the beast just came to somewhere it knew, to a familiar place it stole from your memories. It could have been your home, school, another friend's house. It happened to be here. So what? Just be glad you regained consciousness before . . . before . . ." She can't continue.

I pat Juni's head as she cries. The tears have dried in my own eyes. I'm staring at the dead bodies again, but calmly, detached, knowing what must be done.

"Call Dervish," I tell Juni. "Give him our position. Ask him to bring the Lambs. I won't fight. They can have me. I'll surrender."

"No!" Juni gasps. "They'll kill you."

"They'll exterminate me," I correct her. "And that's what I need. This can't go on. I was wrong to run. I . . ." A thought. "Dervish doesn't know you helped me, does he?"

She shakes her head. "I told him you broke out, that I tried to stop you but couldn't. He took off with the Lambs to track you down. I stayed behind, then sneaked out once they'd left. He doesn't know anything."

"Good. Forget about calling him. I'll do it. Go home and clean yourself up. Say nothing about this to him. You don't have to be involved."

"You don't know what you're saying."

"Yes, I do. This has gone far enough. Too far. I killed tonight. Whether it was me or the beast doesn't matter. We both know that as long as I'm alive, I'll kill again. That can't happen. I won't allow it. So go. Thanks for everything, but I'm past helping." I reach for my phone and start pushing buttons.

Juni gently takes the phone from me. "Come away with me," she whispers. "We'll go where nobody can find us, where you can't hurt anybody."

"What are you talking about?" I frown, trying to get the phone back.

"We'll run," she hisses, holding the phone out of reach. She's stopped crying. Sounds more like her old self. I can imagine her brain whirring behind her eyes. "Head for somewhere secluded and remote. When the next full moon comes, we'll go up to a mountain or into a cave. I'll tie you up and sedate you with magic and drugs to make sure you can't kill anyone. I'll only set you free when the moon has passed. We'll stay in that place and make new lives for ourselves. Keep the world safe from you . . . from the beast."

"You're fantasizing." I sigh. "It wouldn't work. You saw what I did to the cage. I'd escape and kill again."

"No," she insists. "I can control you. I'm sure I can."

"And if I change forever the next time?" I ask. "If the beast takes over?"

"Then I'll do what the Lambs tried to do tonight," she vows. Takes my hands and squeezes. "Don't doubt my conviction. If I have to kill you, I will, regardless of how much that would hurt me. But I don't want to harm you if I don't have to. I still believe that you can be saved. The werewolf should have taken you over tonight but it didn't. You fought it and won. You can win again, I'm sure you can. If I'm wrong . . . if you lose . . ." Her jaw is firm. "So be it. But we have to try. Life's too precious to throw away needlessly."

"I don't know." I look at the bodies again, at Bill-E. "The risks . . ."

"There won't be any," she promises, standing and pulling me up. "We'll leave immediately and find a place where you can't hurt anyone."

I hesitate, torn between knowing the right thing to do and wanting to live.

"If not for yourself," Juni says softly, "do it for me. I love you, Grubbs. Please. Stay alive. For me."

I don't know what to say. I want to go with her. But the beast . . . the magic . . . the murders. I open my mouth, meaning to ask for the phone again, making up my mind to act bravely, selflessly, for the welfare of those I care about.

But what comes out is a weak, "OK. But you have to promise to keep me away from people. And, if necessary, you'll stop me the next time, any way you can."

Juni crosses her heart and smiles. "I promise."

She goes to the back door and opens it, then pushes me ahead of her, out into the night. I stumble through the doorway meekly, silently cursing myself for my cowardice, head low, crying again. Once I'm out, Juni quietly closes the door on the bloodshed and carnage, leaving Bill-E sleeping, to awaken later in the morning to horror and chaos.

FLY ME TO THE MOON

✠ ✠ ✠

JUNI finds a car parked close by. She mutters a quick spell and the doors open. Another spell and the engine fires. She smiles at me through the window and nods for me to get in.

Sitting numbly beside her as she drives. Thinking about the past twelve hours. Studying the blood caked to my hands. Wondering if Bill-E saw me kill his grandparents, if he recognized me behind the mask of the beast. If not, will Dervish tell him? Will he hate me or understand? I think hate. If I was in his shoes, I'd despise the monster who let this happen. No excuses. No forgiving.

Running away is wrong. I've killed Bill-E's grandparents, let Juni wreck her relationship with Dervish, and now . . . what? Drive off into the sunrise, find a sweet little cottage where we can settle down and live happily ever after? Play a warped mother and son game? Let Juni tie me up like a rabid animal every time the moon grows round? Insanity. I should call an end to it now, make Juni stop, hand myself over to Dervish, accept what I have coming.

But instead I sit quietly, staring at the blood or out the window. I try to tell myself I'm doing it because of Juni, that I don't want to hurt her. But that's a lie. I'm running because I'm terrified of being killed. I don't want to let myself be executed. Even though I know, for the safety of everyone I love, that I should.

✠ The car comes to a stop. Juni leans back and sighs, massaging her temples, eyes closed. I look around. We're in a parking lot. Hundreds of cars. A roaring overhead. I lift my gaze and I see a plane come in to land. It clicks — we're at an airport.

"Juni?" I ask quietly.

"Yes," she says, not opening her eyes.

"What are we doing here?"

"We have to get out. They'd find us if we stayed. We need to go somewhere they can't track us. Fly far, far away. It might take three or four flights before we're really safe."

"But I don't have a passport. Luggage. Clothes. Money."

Juni lowers her hands, opens her eyes, and smiles twistedly. "You want to go back to pack a suitcase?"

"Of course not. But how . . . ?"

She rubs her fingers together. "Magic."

✠ Inside the airport. Nobody pays us any attention, even though we're bruised and cut all over, covered in blood. A masking spell. Not that difficult to perform. Even Bill-E's able to cast a lesser masking spell. One of the first tricks any wannabe mage learns.

Juni sends me to the bathroom to get cleaned up. Says she'll meet me by the main departures board in fifteen minutes. Tells me to be careful, not to talk to anyone.

Staring at my reflection in the mirror, eyes dark and ravaged. The hopeless expression of the lost, the damned. Dervish has often said I'm a natural survivor, able to wriggle out of any sticky situation. But sometimes it's not worth wriggling free. What's the point of being alive if you have to live with memories and guilt as crushing as this?

I run hot water and splash it over my face, washing away the worst of the blood. The sink's soon a streaky, pinkish mess. I squirt liquid soap into my hands, clean around the sink, then set to work on myself, scrubbing my hair, taking off my sweatshirt and T-shirt, throwing them into a trash can, washing my upper body and arms. I should get rid of my pants too but I don't like the idea of wandering around in just my boxers. Crazy, considering all that's happened, but some habits are hard to break.

✠ Waiting for Juni. Nervous. Shivering, not from cold but shock. Wanting to call this off. Wanting her to take charge, be a responsible adult, talk me into giving myself up. It's strange how she's acting more irrationally than me. I always assumed mature adults could control themselves better than children, regardless of the pressures. Juni's proving me wrong with every bad call she makes.

"Sorry I was so long," Juni says, coming up beside me, smelling of soap. She looks rough but not desperate. Her eyes are no match for my wild pits of fear.

"Juni, this is crazy, we should —" I begin, but she puts her fingers to my lips before I can continue. Shakes her head lightly.

"Just go with it," she whispers. "I know it's wrong. I know what we should and would do if things were different. But they're not. So let's give ourselves over to craziness and see where it takes us."

Before I can think of a good argument, she glances at the departures board, then leads me to one of the sales desks. I stand behind her as she requests two one-way tickets. No money exchanges hands. Instead, a quick spell and the sales assistant is smiling, handing Juni a pair of tickets, telling her where to check in, wishing her a safe flight and pleasant trip.

Getting in line for check-in. I don't know where we're going — I wasn't paying attention at the sales counter. I think about asking Juni but don't care enough to. What does it matter? We're probably just going to hop straight onto another plane at the next airport anyway. And another after that. Throw the Lambs off our scent. Keep moving until we're safe.

We inch forward. Soon we're at the front. Juni handles the practicalities. No passport? No worries! Not when you use a Juni Swan Confusing Spell™!

Just over an hour's wait once we breeze through security. We spend half of it shopping, replacing our ruined clothes and shoes. I suggest buying extra clothes to change into when these are dirty but Juni says we can restock at the next airport. It'll give us something to do while we're waiting for our connecting flight.

The new clothes feel stiff. The shirt itches, the pants dig

into my stomach, the shoes pinch. But I don't complain. A bit of discomfort is small punishment for the crimes I committed last night.

Sitting on the hard airport chairs. Juni works healing spells, mending the worst of the damage I caused while on the rampage. Her fingers are gentle on my flesh, her voice soft in my ear. Warmth as my cuts stitch themselves closed. Nice.

We're called to board and shuffle on with the rest of the passengers. A large plane. We're twelve rows from the front, seats A and B. When nobody sits in 12C, Juni edges over just before takeoff, so we both have more room. She smiles at me as I stare out the window at the runway, glistening in the early dawn light. I catch her smile in the glass. Turn and smile back. She holds out her hand and I take it.

"All alone now," she says.

"Yes."

"I'm terrified but strangely exhilarated."

"Me too." I give a sickly grin, lying through my teeth. I'm not the least bit excited, only scared, confused, and disgusted with myself for running.

The engines howl. We're pressed back in our seats. *Arrivederci,* terra firma.

✠ Exhaustion kicks in before we reach cruising altitude. My eyelids flutter shut. My brain and body scream for sleep. I try denying myself the pleasure — I want to stay alert in case Juni needs me — but I'm fighting a losing battle.

"It's OK," Juni says, touching my cheek. "You can sleep. I'll watch over you."

"But what if you . . ." I mutter groggily.

"I'll be fine," Juni says. "We both will. Nothing can hurt us now. Not here."

She's right. We're thousands of feet above the Earth and rising. The Lambs can't touch us, not until we land. And with Juni's cunning, I doubt they'll catch us then either. No need for the unease I'm feeling. Better to give myself over to my body's demands and . . . sleep . . . just for a few . . .

✠ Dreams of the cave. The girl's face. Screaming at me. Trying to communicate, to warn me. Frustration in her expression as she realizes it isn't working. I want to understand her, if only to calm her down. But the words make no sense, even in my dream.

Then her face changes. The voice stays the same but it's Juni's face now. She leers at me. A look of vile hatred. It frightens me. I turn to run but Ma and Pa Spleen are there. "You stay away from our Billy," Pa Spleen says, blood gushing from the hole where the right side of his face used to be. "We'll come back and haunt you if you don't," Ma Spleen adds, trying to jam some of her guts back into her stomach.

Whirling away from them. Stumbling for safety. I find Dervish sitting on a stalagmite, looking glum. "You're a fool," he says sadly. "I thought I taught you better. Running away never solved anything. Especially when you don't know what you're running into."

His face changes. He becomes a werewolf. Growls wickedly and leaps. I cringe away from him. Before he strikes, Juni appears and slides between us. She knocks Dervish flat. I rise, shaking, to thank her. But when she turns, there's fire in her pink eyes. "Grubbs," she says, and the word comes out garbled, ragged, as though the lips that formed it aren't entirely human.

The ground rumbles beneath my feet.

✤ I snap awake but the rumbling continues. I sit bolt upright in my seat, not sure if I'm still in the dream, heart racing as it does when I have an especially bad nightmare. I look for Juni but she's not there. The rumbling again. My seat is trembling as if it's about to snap loose from the floor. My insides clench. I feel like something terrible's about to happen. We're in trouble. Where's Juni? I have to find her, save her, get her away from . . .

Nervous laughter. "I'm glad I'm not flying on a full stomach," someone jokes.

"I doubt if anyone will have a full stomach if this keeps up," somebody else replies.

I chuckle and relax. It's only turbulence. We hit another blast of rocky air — *bump!* Groans throughout the cabin. People buckle up their seat belts and sit down if they were standing. Another blast and the whole plane shakes roughly, as if a giant has caught it by the tail and is trying to shake the passengers out. Even the flight attendants make for their seats. That's worrying — it's always a horrible feeling on a plane when you see the professionals acting like there's trouble in store. But it's a normal, human type of worry. No big deal after what I've come through.

I sit back, smiling as kids cry and adults curse. Nervous fliers don't get any sympathy from me. They'll be fine when we pass through this patch of turbulence. Laughing and grinning when we set down. Telling their family and friends about the rough flight, an amusing story in retrospect, fear forgotten by the time they get home. You're never as safe as when you're in the air. Everybody knows that, even if they temporarily forget at moments like this. I bet not one person on this plane will hesitate to fly again, regardless of how much rattling and shaking —

The door to the cockpit blows off its hinges and slams into the people in the first row of seats. Screams of shock and pain. Passengers farther back crane their necks to see what's happening. Some take their belts off and stand, despite the turbulence. Panic is setting in but not taking over. Not yet.

I snap my belt open and slide across to the aisle seat. Where's Juni? Probably in one of the bathrooms. I have to find her immediately. Something bad is happening. I need to get to her so we can face it together.

I'm halfway to my feet when I freeze. I can see into the cockpit from here. Pillars of smoke fill the cabin. My first thought — fire! That would be terrifying enough. But it's not normal smoke. There are strands running from floor to ceiling, left to right, all sorts of crazy angles. Smoke doesn't form in strands. In fact, now that I focus and my brain catches up with what my gut knew the instant I saw it, I realize the pillars inside the cockpit aren't smoke at all.

They're *webs*.

Something small shoots out of the cockpit and attaches itself to the face of a man in the second row. It's the shape of a very young boy, but with too large a head and pale green skin. His scalp crawls with living lice — or it might be cockroaches, hard to tell from here — instead of hair. Fire in the bare sockets where his eyes should be. Mouths in the palms of his hands.

"*Artery!*" I gasp, taking a few automatic steps towards the hell child, numb with shock.

People are *really* screaming now. Those close to the front can see the demon, his teeth, the fire in his eye sockets. Artery rips the man's face off. Blood gushes. Chaos erupts. All the passengers around that row leap to their feet at the same moment and pile into the aisle, getting in one another's way, fighting to race clear of the monstrous baby.

Another demon emerges from the cockpit. This one crawls across the ceiling and drops onto a woman's head. It looks like a giant scorpion but has a face that's almost human. It's bigger than the woman's head. Her neck breaks under the weight. The demon hisses, then strikes the person next to it — a man — with the stinger in its tail. The stinger hits the man's eyes and gouges them out. The demon turns and spits spawnlike eggs into the vacant, bloody sockets. As the man pushes to his feet and screams, some twisted breed of demonic insects hatch from the eggs. They quickly set to work on the flesh around his eyes, spreading like wildfire. Moments later there's not much left of his face and the demon is striking again, this time at a child.

Two more demons spill out of the cockpit, the general shape of humans but covered with boils, gaping sores, and pus. They roar mutely, arms flapping, horrible beasts. They seem to be threatening even more bloodshed and terror than Artery and the other demon — but then they fall to the floor, moaning and thrashing. And I realize they're not demons at all. They're the pilot and one of his crew.

Something leaps over the stricken humans and those milling around the aisle. It lands on top of the seats of the fourth or fifth row. It looks like a rabbit, except with a huge, ugly bulge on its back, and claws that are much bigger than they should be. ("All the better to slice you up with, my dear," a detached part of me giggles hysterically.) The people in the row stare at it, more bewildered than scared. Then it opens its mouth and sprays liquid over them. They fall back gasping and sputtering. Then choked screams as the liquid eats into their flesh, bubbling and boiling, transforming them into mockeries of the human form, just like the pilot and his mate.

I'm standing in the same spot, frozen with fear. Not just fear of what's happened but what I know will happen next. Thinking numbly — *how?* The Demonata shouldn't be able to cross between universes like this. And how did they know I'd be here?

While I'm searching desperately for answers and the cabin around me fills with bodies and screams, a new demon glides out of the cockpit. This one is worse than all the others put together. Tall and thin. Pale red skin covered in smears of blood that oozes from a system of cracks in his flesh. Eight arms with mangled hands — like something a young child might draw — and strips of flesh where his lower legs end. Bald. Dark red eyes with even darker pupils. No nose. A hole where his heart should be, filled with dozens of small, hissing, constantly slithering snakes.

A year after *Slawter,* making good on his vow to track me down and wreak revenge, timing it perfectly for maximum impact and shock, Lord Loss has found me.

"Children," the demon master says, his voice exactly as I remember it, slow and miserable, like he's experienced all the pains of the world. Although he doesn't speak loudly, the word echoes through the plane, right back to the last row of seats. Everyone stops rushing, struggling, fighting, and screaming. All eyes fix on the terrible spectacle hanging in the air just outside the door of the cockpit.

Lord Loss smiles weakly at us as though we'd come to a funeral, only to discover we're the ones due to be buried. "Such a tragic way to die," he murmurs. "Above the clouds. Cut off from the Earth from which you sprang. Most of you without your loved ones. Although isn't it worse if they *are* with you? The pain of dying alone versus the torment of seeing one you love die too." He sighs. "Such a tragedy."

He drifts forward. People slide back into their seats, clearing the aisle, almost hypnotized by the sight of the demon floating towards them. He stops at the third row. There's a young woman in the aisle seat, no more than five or six years older than me. He reaches out with one of his eight clammy hands and strokes her cheek, then gently clasps her jaw.

"If it is any comfort, in this time of great sorrow, I promise your suffering will be short," Lord Loss says, smiling at the young woman. I can see tears in her eyes. His fingers squeeze together tightly. He rips the lower half of her face away and tosses it to Artery, who catches it with the mouths in his hands, snapping it in two and devouring it, yapping like a dog being thrown a tasty tidbit. "But it will be painful," Lord Loss adds with morbid relish.

A child tries to scream. Its father puts a hand over its mouth and cuts the cry short. Everyone's staring at the demon master, transfixed. This is the calm before the storm. Within seconds this cabin will be a place of riotous abandon. But nobody wants to be the first to break the spell. Maybe they — *we* — think that if we stay this way, motionless, barely breathing, the nightmare will pass. The demons won't go wild. We won't all be slaughtered and bled dry by these creatures of evil.

Then — movement behind Lord Loss. Somebody steps forward and looks down the cabin, leaning sideways to see past the demon master. My stomach tightens another notch but I find my voice at last.

"*Juni!*" I shout. "Get away from him! Quick! Before he —"

"Why, Master Grubitsch," Lord Loss cuts in, unable to mask his delight. "*You? Here?* What a delightful coincidence."

Juni slips around the floating demon. Lord Loss takes no notice of her. He only has eyes for me, leering, puffing up his chest, snakes hissing wilder than ever. For a moment I think Juni's cast another masking spell, that he can't see her. Hope flares within me, just the faintest flicker. Then dies just as quickly when she says, "I summoned him, Grubbs."

A chill that is colder than ice. "You . . . ?" I gasp. "*Why?*"

"He's the only one who can cure you," Juni says. "Remember what I said to Dervish? I told him the challenge should be made again. I said you'd be fools not to try."

"What have you done?" I shriek. "We can't bargain with Lord Loss. He won't help us. He'll kill me. He'll kill you. He'll kill us all!"

"Do you know something?" Juni mutters, frowning and

nodding slightly, as if the thought just occurred to her. "I think you're right. With one exception."

There's a man holding a child on Juni's left. Juni reaches across and tries to take the child from the man's arms. He doesn't let go. She tugs but he holds firm. She shrugs, leans in close, and kisses him. I gape at her, bewildered. But confusion quickly turns to terror when I see the man's skin turn grey, then peel away, revealing the blood vessels and bones beneath. He shakes madly but still doesn't let go of the child, who has started to cry.

Juni kisses him relentlessly until there's a sharp snapping sound. She brings her mouth up and his face is attached to hers, head severed at the neck, the remains of his lips snagged between her teeth.

She turns her head aside and spits. Sends the man's head flying to the floor.

Panic erupts. People go crazy and surge down the aisle. The demons snicker and rip into the humans around them with renewed relish. Carnage flowers.

I stand my ground, frozen, more horrified than ever, staring at Juni. She leers at me and wipes her lips clean. Then Lord Loss drifts up beside her. He wraps four arms around the albino and picks her up off the floor. She smiles at him and pecks his cheek, licking a drop of blood clear of the corner of his mouth. Points to me. Grins like a tiger and says, "He's all yours now — *master.*"

TO BE CONTINUED . . .

The bonus chapter for Book 6 could not be printed at this time, as everyone who has read it has met a savage and bloody end, and we don't want to expose any further victims to such a fate.

Proceed at your own risk should you choose to read the next gory installment in the DEMONATA series,

Demon Apocalypse.

Available Now!